YOU CAN'T PREVENT PROPHECY

For Liza, Max, and Rosalie

CHAPTER ONE

The Tomb

"ALL I'M TRYING TO SAY" — Josephus side-stepped an elf's crude overhead swing — "is that if you hadn't lost the map earlier, we wouldn't be in *quite* this predicament."

"Yes, yes," Grilk hissed, pressing its small scaly body against the slick cavern wall. "Hidden entrance or not. Elfs here anyway."

Josephus let out an exasperated sigh, and tossed the long blond hair from his face. "Still" — he kicked a wild-eyed elf to the side — "it would have been a li le easier than this head-on assault." To emphasise the point, he skewered an elf through the back with his sword.

A tumble of rubble pooled at Josephus's feet. At the dim edges of Grilk's torchlight, an inky-dark tunnel lead deeper into the cave network. Three wood-elves emerged, carrying shields and swords, eyes glinting in the flickering light.

"Looks like some of them have a bit of sense left. They've got shields now," Josephus said.

"Elfs no sense. Not trees here. Only rocks."

1

"Maybe they're not wood-elves, maybe they're drow?" His shield blocked an arrow from an unseen a acker. "Can you brighten it up a li le more in here? I can't see where these arrows are coming from."

Grilk's vertical-slit pupils narrowed, the most expressiveness its scaled face could show. "If no light, I see! Tell you where swing. Be er." A flurry of arrows struck the floor around the lizard.

"I know." More arrows whistled past Josephus's ears. Going down on one knee, he tucked himself behind his shield as much as possible. He peered over the steel disc, scanning the nebulous shapes in the dim light. "But don't you think that would be a li le ungainly? Please?" Distress strained his vocal register up an octave as two arrows buried themselves in the metal. "If you would light everything up for just a moment, I can deal with these guys and then we can work out a be er plan."

"Plan good. You bad."

Josephus felt the need to point out — once again — that *he* hadn't lost the map; but another arrow changed his mind. "Please, Grilk. I'll try and do be er next time." Josephus swallowed.

The short, reptilian humanoid snuffled hot air out of its long snout. "Fine," it said. "Be be er."

Grilk raised its arms and allowed the wide sleeves of its cloak to fall into folds by its shoulders. A length of small pockets was strapped along one of its bony arms. The lizard mu ered under its breath and revealed a stone in its upturned palm.

It sounded like nothing more than variously accentuated hisses. Josephus was unsure how to reconcile his lizard companion's abilities with those wizened old men of the magic academy.

Grilk lowered its torch and let the flame lick the stone. The torch went out, its light absorbed by the stone and increased. With a flick of its tail, Grilk leapt into the air, and tossed the stone high. The cavern burst into stark daylight, revealing bright moist rock all around. Stalagmites and stalactites cast shadows against the striated walls. The shield-bearing elves were still outside their tunnel, now shrieking and hissing in the harsh new light.

"There," Grilk said, averting its eyes as the stone fell back to its claw. "Be er for li le man?"

"You're quite a bit smaller than me."

Grilk pull the hood down over its eyes.

Josephus frowned. "Are you alrigh—?"

A gu ural bellow came from behind. He turned to find a male wood-elf running full pelt toward them. When the elf reached the sea of rocks and boulders in the centre of the cavern, he slowed and clambered over them. Then he caught his foot in a crevice.

Josephus scratched an insect bite on his neck. He frowned at the small amount of blood on his finger-tips. "Do you want to handle this one, or should I?" he asked his companion.

"I no want kill," Grilk replied, still fussing with his hood. "Clothes problem."

Josephus nodded and glanced up at the still struggling elf, devoid of the natural grace and poise of its kind. It was a foul magic indeed that had overcome these poor souls. The reptile didn't care, but Josephus didn't relish the unnecessary killing. Though now they were here, there was no sense in going back to find another way through.

"You sure? This one has your name on it?" Josephus

3

teased.

With a stumble, the elf freed himself and careened straight onto Josephus's waiting blade. After a swift cut, Josephus stepped to the side, leaving the elf to tumble face-first to the ground. His severed leg landed with a splash of mud some distance away.

A volley of arrows interrupted Josephus as he prepared to deliver the coup de grâce. Movement high up the vertical wall, where two slabs of rock formed a ba lement, caught his eye. He shooed Grilk up the slope, out of the reach of the partially dismembered elf who still clawed along the ground. Small landslides of pebbles ski ered down the embankment with each footfall.

"Would you mind?" Josephus said, motioning up the w all.

"Grilk do. This. That. Always order. Never ask nice."

"I did ask nicely!"

"Nicer."

Josephus glanced away and rolled his eyes. He turned back to face Grilk, with a beaming smile on his face. "Grilk, would you please be so kind as to assist me with dealing with those wood-elves up there that are a acking us with arrow shot?" Two more arrows dinged into his shield. "I would be ever so thankful and would really appreciate you honouring the blood bond of your chieftain who gave you to me. It would sadden me to have to return you."

"Yes. Grilk do."

A pale blue light emanated from Grilk's hands as it brought them up to its chest. It beat its palms out several times, toward the horizontal slit in the rock. Each thrust hurtled a streaking line of the same pale-blue light towards the source of the arrows. All landed with a blast of blue energy that echoed through the cave, sending shadows dancing in every direction. Sharp cracks accented the explosions, heralding the drop of the slab above, sealing the gap.

Josephus raised his shield over his head and stepped back. The extent of Grilk's magic always surprised him. It was good to have such a stalwart follower on his adventures.

Dust and pebbles rained down from the ceiling as cart-sized boulders fell from the walls and bounded down the slopes. They crashed through columns of rock before coming to rest in the centre, amongst the other chunks of debris.

"Thank you, so, *so* much, Grilk."

Grilk adjusted its hood again, mu ering and cursing, holding the bright stone somewhat behind it. The reptile's voice sounded like rocks grating together.

They continued up the slope of pebbles, toward the opening. The three elves who had appeared ready to a ack, now hung back in the deeper shadows. They brandished their weapons, beating them against their wooden shields, and called out at the would-be assailants.

"What say?" Grilk asked, pointing up at them as it shook a rock free from between its clawed toes.

"I don't know." Josephus pulled a boot free from the deep stones, slipping backwards a li le.

"You say speak elf, liar!" the reptile spat, eyes narrowing again.

"I do speak Elvish." Josephus tried not to lose his patience with his companion. "But *they*" — He pointed his sword up at the elves — "Are not speaking Elvish. They're spouting incoherent nonsense. But that's okay. I'm used to it."

When they reached the top, the elves stepped back. They

5

stood inside the cave, two abreast at the front, the third deeper within. Each of them wore tattered leather armour. These elves would have once been glorious. But the fine leather embroidery had torn, the fastenings tarnished, no longer gleaming with the majesty of elf-kind. One of them wore only a single boot — the remains of the missing one still tightened high under the knee.

Killing them won't get us any answers, Josephus thought. "Ho there," he said with as winning a smile as he could muster between breaths. "What happened here?"

The three elves continued their screeching and yelling, rattling swords and shields.

"I'm here looking for the Eye of Aera'ty Emaryn, you know, the Crystal Singer of Honour Bringing... or something along those lines."

The yelling gave way to grunting — they continued to brandish their arms and armour.

Josephus switched to Elvish. "Right, well... err. It's some sort of medallion, I think," he said, looking down at his reptilian companion. "Right, Grilk? Probably a medallion, or a necklace or..." When Grilk didn't respond he faced the elves. "Well, anyway. There's no need to attack us. We're not interested in whatever weird shit you're doing down here."

The elves renewed their screams, but with a new purpose. One of them threw down his rusted sword, pushed past the others and ran into the tunnel. The other two dropped their weapons and fled. Running footsteps and yelling echoed out of the tunnel.

"This place is weird, Grilk. The sooner we find the thing, the sooner we can be out of here."

"Seem bad?"

"Yeah... but, I'm the Chosen One. Master Thornton told

6

me that we needed to retrieve the Eye to fulfil the prophecy. It's predestined, you know, I practically can't fail."

"You no fail. But what Grilk?"

"I'm sure Master Thornton would've told me if anything bad was to happen to you." He knelt to ruffle the non-existent hair on Grilk's head, but pulled back when the lizard snapped at his hand. "Geez, alright, Grilk. Let's go then." Josephus readied his sword and shield and stepped into the cave. "Can you bring that li le sun-stone with you?" he called back. "It's really dark in here."

PENELLINA DAIRGREN LIFTED HER FOOT over the tripwire that spanned the floor of the crevice. A fallen column sprouted out of the dirt ahead of her, knocked to the side and broken by the weight of the world above. She liked tombs like these the most. Old ones where time had shifted the stonework, making access impossible for the big galoots who lived in this part of the world. But perfect for someone of her stature. She lowered her toe on the other side.

The weight of her backpack shifted, and her back foot slipped out behind her. With flailing arms, she brought everything to bear on her front toe, then tumbled to an awkward rest in front of the wire. It had been raining the last few days; water still seeped through the rock.

She yelped and shook her hand as a millipede a empted to use it as a shortcut, already scolding herself for her reaction. It was not what a master thief would do.

The Eye of Aera was somewhere down in this ancient barrow, at least that's what the people of Barlowe — the nearby human town — seemed to think. If it was down here, she'd find it.

She'd show them. Big people couldn't keep pounding

7

around the world, boasting about how great they were. They didn't even have dancing — except the ungainly stomping and running about which they called dancing.

As she moved further in, the crevice sloped down into the hillside. Light still found its way down here, but the narrow canyon was growing darker.

Penellina hefted the backpack off her shoulders and slung it to the earthen floor. She gave a faint smile as she lifted the flap and rummaged through its contents. The bag was a ta ered old thing — a gift from her grandfather before she left for her adventure. She withdrew a lantern made of wood and brass, le ing her fingers run over the vines and leaves adorning its frame. Her grandmother carved them with great skill and dedication; it was considered a masterwork of her clan.

After lighting the oil wick — from a flint and steel she stole from the general store in Barlowe — she shut the hood, opened the iris, and shone the bright beam of light into the cave. Rocks and moisture glinted back as she picked up her pack and continued forward.

The air was heavy with damp and smelled of wet earth... and something else. Unbidden memories of a dead badger she found when she was a child came to mind. The sight, the smell. It was unmistakable. Her skin crawled. She furrowed her brow more with each step as she strained her eyes and ears for any sign of danger. Anything that was entombed here should have long-since decayed; this was a far more recent death.

She hoped it was just another dead badger.

A padding ahead stopped her in her tracks. She pushed herself against the stone, cursing the overstuffed backpack and its size. The sounds stopped. It was only the echo of her own careless footsteps. This wasn't acceptable for a graceless human or a dwarf, let alone a master thief.

She stopped and checked her surroundings every few feet. At first the beam of light revealed nothing but mud and rock, but now it showed the random pa   ern of cobblestone on the widening floor. The cave wall displayed signs of workmanship too. An outcropping chipped away, an overhang widened to form a rough archway. They confirmed her suspicion: she was entering the tomb proper.

Years of training told her there would be more traps than the tripwire, but she'd seen no further signs. No one ever sets a single trap, there's always a series of them, each more dastardly and deadly than the last.

But they were only a fraction of the risk. Far riskier was whoever set the traps, at least in her experience. The big people in town told her a raging horde of barbaric, elf-like tribesmen protected the place.

She really hoped that wasn't the case.

The clacking of a falling stone froze her in place. She swallowed hard and turned her head to the side, trying to hear any additional sound. When nothing came, she scanned the hallway ahead and reached for the slingshot on her belt. She bent to pick up a stone. How many elf barbarians could she could kill before they swarmed her? Before they tore the limbs from her small frame.

It took a while to gather her courage and will her legs further into the structure. The path ahead continued in a straight line before ending at a wooden door, or at least what was left of one. Inch-thick planks of ro ed wood clung together and held onto two iron hinges for dear life. Judging by the plank's dilapidated appearance, and the soft fragments piled below them, the door wasn't being used to keep anyone out.

Penellina stopped about ten feet from the threshold and regarded it for a few moments. If there was a trap, it would be set on this door. She swung the slingshot and loosed a stone at the bo om hinge. The impact caused the iron to shudder and part from its panel, inducing the plank of sodden timber to shift. Having lost its support, the one above it fell too, which cascaded to the next. Before she knew it, the entire door had fallen into a moist, splintery pile of depressing debris.

Holding the lantern aloft, she tiptoed forward, peering into the interior. Where were the poison darts? The flaming plumes? Had the sound of sodden timber hi ing the stone alerted anyone to her presence? Was that the trap?

Hordes of barbaric elves were make-believe, but someone set that trap earlier. And you didn't set traps unless you didn't want people inside, and if you didn't want people inside you'd lock your doors. Why set a trap and not replace the door with something more substantial?

The answer revealed itself with the sinking of a cobblestone beneath her foot.

"Shitsticks."

She dove forward, hit the ground with her hands, and rolled to the side. A spiked mace swung overhead and clanged against the far wall.

Catching her breath, she waited for the adrenaline to subside, then held the lantern up to inspect the mechanism. Its simple pulley, counterweight, and notched catch revealed that whoever set it had only a rudimentary understanding of mechanics. Just the sort of trap a barbarian elf would make. Maybe the tomb wasn't worth it?

People told tales of the Eye of Aera and its wondrous

value. Enough gold to buy a kingdom. Albeit, a small kingdom, with no castle or keep, but still, there was no way she was going to pass up the chance to return to her clan with a crown on her head. That would really tickle them!

With lantern held out in front, she continued into the darkness. She avoided the larger cobblestones and stuck to the sides. A new hallway branched off to the right, but it was filled with cobwebs and a few too many creepy crawlies.

After a few more steps, urgent footsteps came up behind her. She whirled around and pulled out her dagger. A tall figure ran out from the intersection and crashed into the wall. Its head shook and then snapped to face her. It was an elf, though unlike any she'd seen before. He bared his teeth at her, eyes ablaze with rage, his skin a sickly white.

He sprinted toward her, reaching his arms out.

She turned and fled.

CHAPTER TWO

A Chance Encounter

JOSEPHUS EXPELLED THE SUFFOCATING SCENT of damp air and decay from his nose. Water dripped from the ceiling, threatening to plaster his hair to his scalp. He shied away from the droplets, but there was always another lying in wait.

He rounded a corner through the narrow cave where it opened up, wider than it was tall. Deep, water-cut channels crossed the floor in irregular pa erns. Oddly shaped boulders of smooth rock bulged out at awkward angles. He made a mental note of the way the rocks stuck out, of the smell of the place, the pa ern of the echos — li le details a bard would need when writing the story for perpetuity.

Sheathing his sword, Josephus climbed over the treacherous surface, doing his best to keep the shield out of the way. His hands and boots slipped, jarring his knee against a rock. He tried wedging his hands in one of the cracks, but it was too slimy to provide any extra leverage. Grilk leapt from stone to stone, using all fours to grip the rounded edges.

12

Josephus sighed when his foot slipped into a half-inch furrow of water. "Grilk! Would you keep that sunstone still, please! With all your jumping and prancing I can hardly see where my feet are."

"Walk like Grilk. Hands. Feet. Be er," Grilk said, defying gravity on the edge of a stalagmite.

"Just bring the damned stone closer."

Grilk scampered across the cave floor and tossed the stone toward Josephus. It landed somewhere behind him, bouncing around the rocks before plonking into the water. "Take stone. I see be er."

After rotating himself on the rocks and adjusting his footing, Josephus eyed the water with uncertainty. He scanned the surface for any signs of life before plunging his hand in and yanking the stone out with a splash. "Let's get going then," he said.

As he and Grilk made their way further through the cave, Josephus' eyes widened at the sight of cobblestone and brickwork ahead. "Oh! This must be it," he said while pa ing his pockets. "Excellent."

Grilk ran a finger between two bricks, scraping away the chalking remnants of mortar.

Josephus looked up from the search of his clothing. "Where's the map?"

"I no know."

"That's right. You lost it." Josephus sighed. "Never mind, fate will show us the way."

With proper dungeon flooring now under his feet, Josephus was able to draw his sword and keep it at the ready. There was always an encounter with a creature or two in these old dungeons — he'd been in several the past few years, searching for various prophetic artefacts. He held his shield arm at an awkward angle, trying to cast the light of the stone he held beyond the steel disc.

"Someone come," Grilk said. It seemed bored.

Josephus covered the rock with his fist and set his feet apart. "Grilk, I can't see, it's too dark, do something," he whispered.

"Drop rock. Cast light."

He did. As it fell, its light revealed a tall, thin figure ahead. Ragged clothes hung from the elf's thin frame, a grotesque snarl turned her once beautific features into a bestial visage. She ran toward them and jumped to run along the stonework wall. After two horizontal steps, she pounced, a short-blade pointed toward Josephus.

Josephus arced backwards, stretching his muscles to the limit. The knife passed overhead, followed by the crazed elf. Coming up with his sword, Josephus cut a great chunk of flesh away from her body. She crashed to the floor and rolled some distance before coming to a stop, bucking and thrashing against the stonework.

The elf used one of her jerky movements to lift herself back to her feet. She spun around and snarled at Josephus before charging, both hands pushing her dagger out in front, crimson streams spla   ering on the floor.

Josephus slammed his shield into the oncoming weapon, deflecting it to the side and knocking the elf off balance. His own blade thrust forward, deep into the elf's chest, eliciting a blood-filled groan.

As she slumped into a dying heap, Josephus glanced the way she had come. "Thanks for the help, Grilk." He looked back the other way, toward the cavern. "Grilk? Where are you?"

When no reply came, Josephus furrowed his brow.

"Where did you go?"

He retrieved the sunstone and proceeded as before, casting an eclipse of his shield before him. After thirty feet, the stonework improved. The walls were now covered in a concrete render, though it had crumpled and fallen in patches over time. Chunks of it accumulated in the narrow gu ers along the bo om of the walls.

Grilk's voice echoed from the hallway ahead. "Trip-wires. Be careful."

"What trip—"

Josephus felt something catch his boot and looked down in dismay at the silvery glint of a trip-wire. "Oh fu—" A swinging stone, suspended by ropes, hit him from the back, knocking the wind out of him. His sword fell with a cla er as he stumbled to the wall. Wincing, he rotated his shoulder and felt something creak inside.

"That trip-wire."

The stone spun on its rope in front of Josephus. Squiggles of writing was carved into the surface — somewhat like the flowing script of elves, but poorly done, like a child's. He couldn't decipher it. He picked up his sword, got to his feet, and frowned at the stone. Something like this shouldn't have befallen the Chosen One, but he supposed there needed to be some sense of danger to make a good story.

Another twenty feet brought the hall to an end. A rusty portcullis blocked a doorway ahead. The metal bars showed scratched silver lines down through the rust, beyond which was a large room. In the centre stood Grilk, gazing up at the ceiling, scratching the underside of its snout.

"Did you close this door?" Josephus asked.

"Close by self. Come."

Josephus gripped a horizontal length of metal along the

15

bo om of the bars and hefted. The gate remained as it was.

"Can you help me open this door please, Grilk?"

Grilk walked over to the bars and looked around the walls on his side. "Rope broken. No help."

"Can you cast a spell please? Just, you know, melt the bars or something?"

The small reptile reached a claw into the folds of its cloak. It withdrew a dirty, yellowish lump.

"Is that... bu er?"

"Yes. For spell."

"Did you take that from Master Thornton?"

Rather than respond, Grilk started the hissed mu erings of one of its spells. It waved the bu er in a circle as it stepped forward, then pressed the goop against each of the bars. By the time it was done, there was no bu er left in its claws. Grilk stepped back, apparently happy with its work.

"Is that it?"

"Yes. Lift."

Josephus did as instructed. He raised his eyebrows in disbelief as the gate slid into the ceiling above. He gave his companion a li le nod. "Thank you, Grilk."

Once through the gate, Josephus lowered it to the ground and scanned the room. Four plinths dominated the space, positioned at equal distances from the walls and each other. The smashed remains of marble busts — no doubt having once sat proudly upon the plinths — now lay sca ered on the floor. He flipped a few pieces over with foot and sword-tip.

"They look more like men than elves. Definitely not dwarfs. I wonder why these silly elves are down here. There isn't a forest for miles."

Josephus pointed Grilk to the only door available to

them, waited for the lizard to proceed, and then followed. The new hallway appeared identical to the one a ached to the cave, complete with trickles of water which were impossible to navigate around. Grilk tipped its head back, opened its long snout, and drank from one of the constant streams.

"That water is filthy, Grilk. There's no telling what kind of diseases you're subjecting yourself to. Yours really are a dirty people."

When Grilk had satiated its thirst, it responded, while standing in the stream. "Water clean. Rock filter. Pure." Its dark grey cloak was covered in mud and muck from the flow of water.

Josephus shook his head. What was the best way to educate his companion? The cloak was a gift he'd given the reptile when it was first rewarded to him by its tribe. An a empt to civilise it, or at least hide its reptilian appearance while in town. Not that the ruse ever worked, someone always spied a snout, claw, or yellow eye. When they got back to Master Thornton in Threerun, he'd buy Grilk a tent or bedroll. Something the creature could camp in while Josephus was in town. Somewhere secluded.

Ahead of them came faint whispers of metal and footfalls.

"This is it, Grilk. The main chamber is up ahead, this is where we should find the Eye. I'll rush in. You come in behind and blast anything that looks threatening. Okay?"

"Grilk blast. You wait."

"No no. I'm the Chosen One. I'll go. Don't worry, I won't be hurt. Just wait a minute before coming in."

Josephus's face contorted into a grimace as he brushed aside a wet muck that hung from the ceiling. It stuck to his

17

shield and slapped down over the edge, weing his exposed forearm. He shivered and tried to fling it off, but it only seemed to wrap around his skin more.

When he entered the next chamber, still trying to rid himself of the sludge, he paused and cocked his head to the side. There were three more elves here, all male, facing away from him and standing around a pedestal. They grunted and snarled at each other in various timbres and pitches, gesticulating wildly. Half-plate armour — steel breastplate and pauldrons held together with leather — adorned them. At their sides hung sheathed longswords.

Josephus waved the stone around a lile. When they didn't react, he took a tentative step closer. Then another. He stepped forward with more certainty, to get a beer look at the object on the pedestal.

A golden necklace hung, suspended in the air, as though held by an invisible hand. Sparks of light glinted off the chain as it slowly rotated. At the base of the chain was an oval shaped seing with a large gem inside. It looked very much like an eye. The stone glinted blue and then green, shifting colours with every movement of light.

With a frown, Josephus regarded the three arguing figures once more. They still hadn't noticed his approach.

"Ahem." Josephus coughed. "I take it *that* is the Eye of Aera?"

The closest elf pivoted his head and hissed. Josephus kept his sword pointed at them and moved closer still. The elf made a guural sound, somewhere in the back of his throat — the most un-elf like sound Josephus had heard one make. Though considering how un-elf like they appeared, it didn't surprise him. In response, the other two elves moved forward and hissed as well.

With the surety that prophecy protected him, Josephus took one final step forward. The three elves moved in unison, stepping to surround him, wielding their swords with both hands.

Josephus ducked and held his shield overhead as all three blades came swinging down on top of him. Seeing an opportunity, he hacked at a cloth covered leg and rolled himself clear. When he bounced to his feet he broke into a wild smile.

Elvish steel flashed again, this time with a straightforward thrust. He parried the blade, sending it spinning to the ground. Not allowing the glinting metal to distract him from the task at hand, he thrust and pierced the elf through the chest.

The elf's body had not yet touched the ground when Josephus was beset again. He disarmed both a   ackers with a single parry, and then countera   acked. Two elvish heads rolled along the ground, trailing a bright red line behind them. Josephus smiled as he wiped his blade on one of the bodies' tunics.

"Eye now, we go," Grilk said. It was standing near the doorway of hanging muck, snapping up and pulling bits down to slap against its head.

As Josephus moved to investigate the hovering necklace, something small ran into the room from a previously unnoticed doorway, carrying a light. Without stopping, it disappeared behind a thick curtain of cobwebs and hanging moss. The light disappeared. Using his sword, he swept some of the webs away, searching for the intruder, but found only bare floor.

"Grilk, did you see what that was?"

Something grunted behind him. He whirled around,

19

holding his sword at the ready. An elf crumpled to the ground. Behind it stood a small woman, about Grilk's height, with a shocked expression on her face, breathing heavily. A travelling cloak lay across her shoulders and an over-sized backpack sat on her back. In one hand she held a blood stained knife, in the other, a small lantern. She frowned and studied her blade and the dead elf, then looked up at him with a smile.

"Hello, um…," she said, bending to wipe her blade on the elf's rags. "He was going to kill you. I killed him. I saved you."

"Indeed," Josephus said, sheathing his sword. "Come, Grilk," he called out to the passageway behind her. "I've got the Eye."

"Oh, is that the Eye?" The small woman leaned to see past him. "It's very pre y, can I take a look?" She pushed her hair out of her face and brushed past his hip.

"I am Josephus, the Chosen One."

"Wow, good for you. I'm Penellina, you can call me Penny if you like" — she reached up on her tiptoes to get a be er look at the necklace — "most of you big people do. How does it hover?"

"Some kind of magic is in this place. Most wicked and dangerous."

"It doesn't look dangerous," she said, reaching a hand out.

Josephus snatched the necklace before Penellina's fingertips reached it. "It is. I need it to fulfil the prophecy."

"What about traps?"

"What about them? The ones here are hardly dangerous." He flicked his hair and smiled down at her. "At least not dangerous for me."

As he smiled down at her, a deep rumble reverberated

around the room. Li le columns of dirt cascaded from the ceiling as cracks spread in chaotic steps across it.

The small woman yelled and pushed at his hips. "Run! Run! It's a cave-in trap."

"Is it? What's a cave-in trap?" Josephus asked. Though she wasn't able to move him, she had more strength than he thought.

"We'll be crushed!"

A chunk of rock, large enough to crush a chosen one, fell on the pedestal, obliterating it. A mass of dirt followed it, funnelling into the room from the new hole. Josephus found himself trying to recall any stories where the hero died. The wall behind him caved in. It was time to leave.

He indicated the portcullis and watched the halfling dodge falling stones as the ceiling fell apart. Josephus jogged forward when another large rock crashed a few feet away. The thunderous cracks of earth overwhelmed all other sound.

"Allow me," he yelled over the din, giving a flourished li le bow. He hoisted the bars up.

The halfling ducked through the opening the moment she could fit. Josephus gave a li le yelp as another large section of the ceiling fell down next to him.

"It's really quite okay!" His voice broke a li le as he lifted the iron bars over his head. As he stepped through, the remainder of the ceiling caved in with a resounding boom. Dust and dirt billowed up and drowned out the light from the sunstone.

Josephus waved his hand near his face, squinting against the dust. "I'm the Chosen One. I can't fail. You're in no danger while you're with me. It's all in the prophecy."

Penellina coughed. "Prophecy?" She rose to her feet,

dusting her arms and legs.

"Yes, the prophecy of Azair Soloth. I'm the Chosen One, destined to quell the evil that arises in these lands."

She looked at him with an encouraging smile that broke through her thick covering of dirt, waiting for him to say more. Josephus looked down at his own clothes and tried to brush some of the earth away. This wasn't a good look for a hero.

"Where is he?" Josephus turned. "Gril— oh there you are."

Grilk emerged from the shadows and dust. He was free of dirt. "Have Eye. We go."

"Do you have a cleaning spell, Grilk?"

It looked at him, both hands hidden in the cloak's over-long sleeves. "Why?"

Josephus felt his face redden the dust as he looked at Penny apologetically. "It's just that I'm sure Penny here would rather not be covered in dirt." *And this is no way for a hero to be seen.*

She looked down in surprise and shook the fabric of her trousers. "I don't mind," she said. "Just a bit of dirt."

"No, no. Please, allow me," Josephus held a hand out. "Grilk, you are to clean us both, at once."

"I no know spell for clean. Only dirty."

"Really, Grilk. You are impossible." He lowered his voice and stepped closer. "You are embarrassing me." He turned to Penny. "I'm so sorry. He's not usually this disagreeab—"

"—can I come with you?" Penellina asked.

Josephus smiled at her tactful change of subject. "What are you doing down here anyway, a li le woman like you?"

"Well... I'm lost. I got separated from my friends. I tried to take shelter in a cave, and I found these hallways" — she gestured around — "heard a ruckus, and came across you about to be dead. I saved you."

Josephus had been waiting for this moment; the moment where he earned his second trustworthy companion. Every heroic adventurer ended their quest with multiple followers. He was well on his way now. "It must be fate. I'll take care of you, please, travel with us."

"Thanks!" She stepped up to Grilk. "What is it?" she asked, peering at the lizard.

"That's Grilk, my... servant. Its people owed me a life-debt, and so I take care of it. Be careful, it tends to bite."

PENELLINA DANCED FROM SIDE TO side to avoid the drips of water as she followed the blond-haired dope. He had stashed the golden necklace into a large bag on his belt, but the knot he used to secure it was nothing. She could untie it and lift the Eye that way, or a smooth slice from her dagger could get her the entire bag — it might have something else valuable in it. But she'd have to wait until they got out of here. She only got the drop on the elf that chased her after it stopped to a ack this fool, she didn't want to take on another by herself.

The fool stopped suddenly and faced her. When he saw where she was looking, he glanced down. "Oh, no," he said, his voice grave. "Do you know how to lift that?"

"What?"

"That stain." He pulled out his leather armour toward her, kneeling down a li le to give her a be er view. "It's blood, or mud, or something."

"I'm sure it will come out with a li le elbow grease," Penellina said. "So... um. Josephus. You said you're the Chosen One?"

"Yes, as foretold by the prophecy of Azair Soloth." He

stood and adjusted his leather before walking on.

"Who's she?"

"*He* is the greatest prophet of the elven conclave of O'erthe in Rivendale."

Penellina frowned. It was just like humans to be weirdly dogmatic about drug-induced hallucinations from elven mystics. They were supposed to be interpreted, not taken literally. Hells, she could predict the future too if she had nothing to do but lie about and get spiritual. "Right, that's great! So um... What do you need the Eye for?"

The young halfling didn't miss the almost imperceptible turn of Grilk's head in front of them.

"Be er woman go ahead. Easier to protect," it said.

"Yes, yes. Good thinking, Grilk." Josephus stopped and let Penellina ahead of him. "It is one of the items I need to extinguish the evil in these lands."

"We can't have evil sprouting up." She shook her fist. "How will it help?"

The man's footsteps behind her slowed. She glanced back at him, he seemed troubled. He sped up again, faster than before. "It will all become clear once I return it to Master Thornton."

"Where is he?"

"In Threerun."

A wry smile broke Penellina's frown. Threerun was to the east, but she was going west. Back to Barlowe, that town of even bigger, even dumber men, so she could rub their noses in it. "Oh, that's a coincidence! My friends and I were coming from Threerun, I'm sure I'll find them back there, safe and sound."

"I don't think your friends are real," Josephus said.

Penellina felt cold sweat on the back of her neck. She

summoned as much innocence as she could. "What do you mean?" She searched the area ahead for a retreat.

"Any friends that abandon the search for you are not true friends."

A warm feeling of relief washed over her. "Yeah. You're probably right. Still. That's where I'm heading. To Threerun, back to my home. Everyone knows that when they're looking for Penny, they'll find her in Threerun."

"Odd. I've spent many years in Threerun with Master Thornton. I don't remember seeing many half-men. Where in Threerun do you live?"

The grip of panic returned. "Um... yeah. We uh... we don't go out much. Most of you big people are very unkind to us." She added a hint of righteousness to her voice. "'Half' men. We're not half as good as you, you know."

"Yes, I figured as much."

"I half be er than all you," Grilk added ma er-of-factly. "Twice be er than half-man."

"Half-*woman*," Penellina corrected him. She let out a silent breath when they didn't push the topic any further.

When the worked stone of the hallway gave up and succumbed to natural rock, the li le lizard person hopped away, darting over boulders at the edges of the light. Though Penellina still carried her lantern, she extinguished it when they first set out together. The li le orb of radiance Josephus carried illuminated enough, no sense in wasting good oil.

She stopped and waited for Josephus to go first.

"No, no. Please, after you," he said, gesturing grandly.

"Oh, no. You go ahead, it might take me a while."

"All the more reason for me to stay behind you, in case you need my assistance. Those rocks really are quite precarious."

There was no way she was going to stay ahead where he could monitor her. "Yeah, but I need you to go first so... that I can see how it's done." She smiled at her own cleverness.

Penellina waited for Josephus to go first. He stumbled and slipped over the rocks, banging a knee here and an elbow there. A laugh pushed its way out of her throat, but she managed to hide it under a cough.

"Is everything alright?" Josephus asked, stopping to study her.

"Yeah, fine, fine. I'm just a li le sad that my friends left me. You've given me a lot to think about."

He frowned gravely at the rocks between them, then with a solemn nod, turned and resumed his haphazard climb.

"Maybe half-one sick," Grilk said from the darkness ahead. "Medicine."

"Yes, yes. Good idea, Grilk." Josephus swung the pack off his back. He rummaged through it and pulled out a small vial of brown liquid. "Here, this will set you right as rain," he said, holding it out.

"Err, what is it?" she asked.

"Mrs Hammersmith's Cure-all," he told her. "Good for what ails you."

She took the vial and downed it. The flavour was a combination of every overcooked vegetable she'd ever eaten, with a hint of pine. It was thick enough that she was forced to chew it, but it reformed whenever the pressure from her teeth let off. She swallowed the slimy lump whole and felt a perverse sense of pride in not gagging.

"Thanks," she said, coughing.

"You've a stout heart!" Josephus said as he continued on. "I've never been able to stomach the stuff."

Penellina sighed and walked from rock-tip to rock-tip, arms held out to catch her balance when needed. She was ge ing used to the pendulum-like weight of the backpack, but there were a lot of new movements to learn. When she returned to her clan, she'd organise some of the training to be done with weights — it's a lot different sneaking about with a *laden* pack.

She was careful to remain behind Josephus and keep an eye on him. Every time he watched to see how she fared, she would fall to her bo om, or ensure she had four limbs on the rocks. The lizard was at the end of the cave now, si ing and waiting. It must have felt as frustrated as she did at the slow pace.

When they reached the edge of the cave, Josephus smiled and spoke to her. "Through this next bit of cave, the tunnel opens up into a large cavern. The exit is on the opposite side, at the bo om. Do you need help ge ing down?"

"Okay. Thanks," she said. It was hard to swallow her pride.

"Can we use your rope there? I didn't think to bring one. We can tie it to these pointy rocks in here, it looks long enough to get you to the base of the cavern."

Penellina paused for a moment. She didn't want to lose her rope, it cost almost two gold pieces. But if she wanted to rob this idiot she needed to appear feeble. She bit her bo om lip. There had to be a way out of it.

She relented. "Yeah, thanks. I'm not sure how I'd manage otherwise."

When she tried to remove her backpack to detach the rope from its side, Josephus waved her hands away. "Allow me," he said, turning her around. After he'd detached the rope, he tied an amateurish knot before he disappeared

27

through to the cavern. "Just around this corner and I can lower you down."

The lizard remained si ing, watching her with an expressionless face. She examined the hoop of rope thrown over a stalagmite and humphed. He would likely insist on lowering her down, but that knot would never hold.

With deft hands, she untied the knot and remade it the way her grandfather had shown her. Nodding at her own work, she looked up. The reptile-man still watching her. "What?" she asked. "That would never have held. And I get my rope back this way." She walked past with her chin held high.

Around the corner, she found Josephus handing her another loop of rope. "Here, put this under your arms. If you walk backwards, I can gradually lower you."

"Thanks so much for this. I really appreciate it. I'm sure my family in Threerun will reward you."

"I don't do it for reward. Don't worry, it's all part of the plan. You'll be a part of my courageous entourage, trekking through dungeons and the wilderness, seeking out adventure on our quest. Fate has brought us together."

For a moment, Penellina wondered whether the Eye was worth it. No, no. It was worth it. Rather than continue the conversation, she stared at her feet and the stones. She made agreeable sounds as he continued speaking, wishing he would stop. He was lowering her down a rocky slope, steep enough that an inexperienced climber could call it a cliff. To the side, a mound of pebbles formed a sort of natural slide. *We could have slid down there on our bums.* She grit her teeth at the slow descent.

Once she reached the bo om, she freed herself and waved up. Josephus nodded and made his way to the slip of rocks. He sat down and pushed himself off the edge, sliding sideways in a rain of stones and dust. When he reached the bo om, he took two steps to catch his speed and spun to face her. He smiled expectantly. She said nothing.

She gave the rope two tugs and started reeling it in over her elbow.

"It's firmly a ached up there," he said. His tone annoyed her.

Keeping her eyes on him, she continued to reel it in. When it was evident she had pulled down more rope than she should have been able to, he frowned.

"Odd. I swear that was tied securely."

"Good thing you didn't drop me. Just when I was thinking you were a friend." She pouted her lips and averted her eyes.

His frown deepened, but he said nothing more. Instead he made his way across the boulders in the centre of the cavern, toward sunlight coming from around a bend.

When they reached what she assumed was the exit, he turned to wait for her once more. "Penny?"

"Yes, Josephus."

"How did you know that the pedestal was trapped?"

"I... ah... I didn't. Not really. It's just... something I remember from a story my grandmother told me."

His face lit up. "She told you stories of the Azair Soloth prophecy?"

"Yeah, nah. Only that the treasure is always booby-trapped."

That seemed to satisfy his curiosity, or at least shut him up.

Once they were outside, they found it was almost dark, the sun a warm hazy memory in the distant plains.

Overhead the stars were twinkling through gaps in the cloudy sky. These fell lands were rocky and barren, a few scrubby bushes and dead trees do ed what li   le landscape they could see. Everything was grey or brown, and very dull.

"We should have good weather tonight," Josephus said. "We'll camp here. Grilk can set some alarms around us." He surveyed the immediate area around them and then studied the entrance to the cave. "Where is he?"

"Here. Come. Good spot," Grilk said, approaching them from the side of the hill.

They followed it to an overhang of rock, with smooth stone inside, and deep sandy dirt covering the ground. She set her bedroll down a li   le way from the fire Josephus built, preferring to remain in partial shadow. When Grilk made weird gestures she kept note of where he stood each time. Although she didn't have a lot of experience with magic, she knew a practitioner when she saw one. Her clan had taught her well.

Rather than eat or talk, she feigned sleep and imagined all the things she would do with a kingdom's worth of gold. A human registry for one, keep tabs on them. Maybe tax them a bit more too, she didn't want too many of them se ing up shop in her lands. They were so loud and obnoxious, never considering the other races.

She fantasised well into the night before rising quietly. With careful steps and shallow breaths, she relieved Josephus of the Eye and made her escape toward Barlowe.

CHAPTER THREE

The Three Dancers

FARALD WAITED FOR HIS MEAL in the common room of The Three Dancers Inn, enjoying the night's entertainment — a wrestling tournament. The current bout was between a farmer and a blacksmith if his guess was right, the size of a man's forearms told you a lot about him. The opponents manoeuvred around each other before a few quick moves sent them stumbling and grappling in the direction of his table. Farald lifted his mug as other ones jumped or fell to the floor. Cheers erupted from the onlookers as the farmer kicked the feet out from under the smithy and dove on top of him. The table creaked in protest.

As near as Farald could tell, the common-folk of Barlowe fought until one of them cried out in pain. In his travels through the kingdoms, he'd never seen it done quite like this. In Lavender, a referee called when the fight was over, and in Ableview the wrestling only ended when the crowd got bored.

Farald looked for somewhere out of the way to enjoy his

31

meal. Aside from the few logs carefully rationed in the fireplace, there was a single candelabra — with only half the candles lit — hanging near the bar. The poor light hid every corner in darkness, though Farald's dwarven eyes had no trouble penetrating it.

More than a few unscrupulous types were gathered in one of the dark corners, talking in hushed tones. Some of them carried blades, and some of them had ta oos down their arms. A scar carved its way across their leader's face. All were the kind of men too lazy to make a good go at honest work, preferring the more immediate profits of banditry — he'd come across the type plenty of times over the years in human lands. The farmers and tradesman — the people Farald preached to after his arrival this morning — had the foresight to stay clear of the bandits. They gave him a wide berth, too. Despite being willing to worship nearly any god, humans never met religious conversion with open arms.

The usual tavern sca ering of tables and chairs was pushed aside, into tighter clumps, to make room for the wrestling. At this late hour, most of the tables were wet with spilt drinks, though the innkeeper's boy rushed around mopping up as best as he could. Farald chose one of the drier tables.

"We'll have none of your bullshite in here, tonight, master dwarf," the innkeeper stated. He slid a trencher heaped with food under Farald's nose — root vegetables, gravy, meat, bread. "I don't want you scaring off my customers with your talk of dwarven gods."

"God. Just the one." Farald straightened the trencher in front of him. "And Whurgan Ellagg is not just the god of dwarves, he's the god of all strong people. You know, you look to be a strong fellow yourself, have you thought about your eternal soul recentl—"

The innkeeper dismissed him with a wave and walked back to the kitchen. It hardly ma ered whether the man listened or not. There were a hundred thousand souls in The Three Kingdoms. Farald didn't need to convert them all.

Hoots and laughter rose up as the blacksmith twisted the farmer's arm behind his back. Ale sloshed out of tankards as the onlookers raised them into the air, celebrating the sound of his pain. Copper pieces exchanged hands.

While the next two combatants were being called — there appeared to be a roster — the brass bell above the door rang. It was late, closer to sunrise than sunset.

A young halfling woman strode in. She held her head high and her back straight against the obvious weight of her pack. Her boots were mud-covered, and her cloak looked a li le worse for wear. An adventurer. Li le chance for conversion — they rarely cared to consider what happens after death.

She shrugged her backpack off and jumped onto the closest table, ignoring the patrons using it and her own mud-caked boots. "A ention, you big people!"

The dull roar of conversation and jokes remained constant.

"I have done what you all said was the impossible!" She flourished her arms. "Even though you all said it couldn't be done!"

Two people at a nearby table looked up at her. The woman and man si ing at the table she stood upon tried to push her legs to the side to continue their conversation.

"I have the Eye of Aera!"

Farald stopped chewing and set his knife and fork down. The Eye of Aera was thought to be lost, and thankfully so. It contained a distillation of some of the most powerful magic

33

which ever existed, that of the old god of the elves. A hundred of Aera's disciples channelled their divine powers into it, for what purpose they never indicated, but it destroyed them and their church. Destroyed a whole mountain, if he remembered correctly.

Whurgan Ellagg would embrace him once again if he secured something as powerful as the Eye.

The halfling reached into her cloak and produced the item, holding it aloft for all to see. Few people paid her any a ention, though one of the louts in the corner nudged his mates at the display of gold. There was more wealth in that necklace than in the entire town, more wealth in that necklace than she had sense — waving it around like that.

Her smile creased into a frown after a few moments of being mostly ignored. At the insistence of the people below her, she jumped down from the table. Struggling to gain the innkeeper's a ention, she climbed up a stool at the bar to shout. When he'd finished serving everyone else, he handed her a mug of ale. She took a long gulp and sat it down with a sour face, eyeing the cup's contents with a raised brow.

Farald took his mug and, having lost his appetite, left his half-finished meal behind. He took the long way around, giving the wrestlers as much distance as possible. As he moved along, three of the men in the corner got up and walked out the front door, trying not to look at the halfling. Farald took a seat next to her. She was fastening the chain of the Eye around her neck.

"I think you're in a bit of trouble," Farald said.

"Oh?" She looked away.

"That's a lot of gold you just showed everyone."

That got her a ention. "You mean The Eye of Aera. You know they said it couldn't be recovered from the tomb? I recovered it. It's mine. I got it." She looked around before leaning in and winking. "I had to kill a shit-load of elves to get it."

Farald gave her a tight smile. "Is that so?"

She nodded.

"Well, it's not going to be yours for long."

Though she tried to keep it subtle, her free hand move down to the scabbard at her belt. Farald raised his hands in supplication.

"All I mean is, you've caught the a ention of a few people who won't have any problem taking it from you. They'll kill you if needs be, no ma er how many elves you say you've killed." He subtly pointed in the general direction of the three remaining ruffians in the corner.

She turned as though to watch the wrestling, bringing the mug up to her lips. "I'm not worried about those bums."

The li le bell above the door rang again. A blond-haired man entered. There were dark bags beneath his eyes and his hair was in disarray. Under the leather armour, his chest heaved with exertion, and sweat lined his brow. The innkeeper greeted him as the man slung a backpack onto the floor. It landed with a heavy thud. Farald was sure something moved under the fabric.

The man's smile was the white-toothed kind that only wealth and a city upbringing could give you. He turned to lean against the bar and survey the room. His eyes narrowed as they fell on the halfling.

"Penny!" he said, slamming his fist on the bar. "My considerable skill will allow me to track you no ma er what lies you weave. Give me the Eye."

The small woman turned mid-drink. She coughed foam and ale as her eyes widened. "Shit," she mu ered, grabbing

35

her backpack and pelting for the kitchen.

As she took flight, the three ruffians made their move, rushing to position themselves between her and escape.

"Oh, you bastards," she yelled at them. "You're all in it together, keeping the li le man down!"

"Give me the Eye, Penny." The blond approached behind her, his hand rested on the hilt of his sheathed sword. "You don't know what you're doing. Its magic is corrupting your feeble mind."

Farald stood — as did many of the carousers — and stepped out of the way as the spokesman of the three ruffians voiced his opinion.

"We saw it first there, mate. You stay back." He looked at the woman. "Give us that gold, darling. We won't hurt you."

The halfling looked like a frightened animal before flight or fight kicked in. She chose flight. Straight at Farald.

She stepped up a chair as she ran, riding its pinnacle as it toppled forward. At its zenith she leapt to a table, her feet pounding along the top — eliciting cries of indignation — then launched herself to the bar.

Her boots landed with a short skid on the wet surface. Farald caught her with one arm as she fell, lifting the long necklace off her thin frame with the other. He turned with her momentum and set her down — li le feet still running along. It took a few steps before she realised what he'd done.

"Hey! Give that back you fuckin'… fat midget!"

"I'm sorry. I think it's best if I take it."

"Thank you, dwarf!" The blond walked towards him with a wide smile and wide arms. "She burgled that from me some hours ago. I'm glad to have it back."

"I'm sorry. I think it's best if I take it."

"Oi! Give us that gold, or we'll fuck you up."

The group of louts fanned out.

Farald held his hands out, appealing for calm. "I'm sorry. I think it's best if I take it. This is a powerful artefact, thought lost to the world. I'll take it to my church where my god can keep a watchfu—"

A clay mug whistled past his head — the halfling was reaching for a plate next. The three hoodlums charged him, tables and chairs crashed out of their way.

Farald sighed.

As the first fist came at him, Farald stepped to the side. His sudden movement threw the a acker off balance, opening their ribs to a swift strike. A chair broke against Farald's arm as he blocked the second man. Steel flashed in the corner of his eye. He turned in time to meet the blade, pushing it to the side with his arm and knocking its owner's teeth out.

"Alright. Let it go, boys. You're no match for me," Farald said.

The front door banged against the wall as the other three bandits re-entered. They carried chipped swords and rusty shields. One wore a dusty helm, cobwebs still hanging from it. On the ground around Farald the other three were pulling themselves together.

"Thank you again, dwarf." The blond was still smiling. "Of course, I would have handled that a li le be er. But still, well done." He held his hand out as he approached.

Farald took a step back, raising his palm once again. "Like I said, I think it's best if I keep a hold of it."

The man's smile collapsed into a frown. He drew his sword. "That is regre able. I am Josephus, the Chosen One, of the Azair Soloth prophecy. I'd have your name before I defeat you."

37

Of course, the Azair Soloth prophecy required the Eye… there was another prophecy too, wasn't there? Farald's thoughts were interrupted by the sudden crockery flying around him. His own knife and fork cla   ered to the ground at his feet. In the corner of his eye, he caught the halfling scurrying around for more projectiles.

The ill-kept swords entered the fray with half-remembered ba   lecries from childhood stories. Though they came for Farald, his blond opponent stepped to meet them. He parried the first sword and knocked the second out of its owner's hands. The third stopped short and backed away.

Rapid footsteps from behind brought Farald's a   ention to the fleeing halfling. The fine golden chain dangled from his hand, but the Eye was gone. She came to a stop in front of the kitchen door, frozen in mid stride, her fist gripping the gold se   ing with gem.

Before Farald could determine what happened, a fist connected with the back of his head. He shook the encroaching blurriness from his eyes and started swinging. His elbow caught a body, his knuckles struck a face, he stumbled. Something wooden broke across his back. He was beset from all sides and pummelled to the ground.

The assault stopped with someone's scream of pain. Eager to fight on, Farald rose to his feet, shaking confusion from his head. The blond swordsman was nearby, thrusting his sword at the array of ruffians surrounding them both.

Feet hammered along the wooden floor as a mass of farmers, bakers, and tanners crashed between them and started swinging. Farald took a step backwards and opened himself up to the oncoming men. He lifted the first one, feeling the sting of a blade across his shoulder, and tossed him to the side. His fists slammed into the arms and torso of another as he kicked back a third. Behind him, the sounds of steel meeting steel rang out.

Farald whirled and rushed at the blond's back. Just as he was about to tackle him, someone shoved Farald to the side. He took an elbow to the nose, filling his eyes with tears. After striking a man next to him, Farald kicked the back of a knee in front. One of the men screamed while the other laughed. Farald grabbed their two heads and slammed them together.

The blond was in front of him now, stepping quickly into range. Farald grabbed a table leg and readied it against the oncoming blade. The blond brought the sword down in an overhead swing but a chair broke across his back, sending him sprawling. Farald ignored him and kept fighting, punching at everything and everyone that came within range.

When the fight was over, Farald looked around him. Some men groaned and crawled to safety. Others lay unconscious or worse. Furniture rested on its side or sat in cracked heaps. The floor was wet with puddles of ale and blood. He winced as he rotated his cut shoulder. Something in the joint clicked back into place.

Remembering the blond, Farald looked around the room. He was by the halfling, prying her fingers from the Eye. She remained like a statue in mid stride.

"What are you doing?" Farald said, stomping over. "It really is best if I take—"

His forward momentum stopped. Looking down, his feet dangled an inch from the ground. To his left a voice hissed harsh consonants. With great effort, he turned himself in the air.

Standing by the bar was a small, cloaked figure. From the darkness within the hood, a scaled snout protruded. Above it, two yellow, serpentine eyes glowed. Farald swallowed hard.

PENELLINA WATCHED JOSEPHUS AND GRILK walk out through the kitchen with the Eye. The sudden introduction of magic into the melee quickly put an end to the hostilities. Any wrestlers who were still standing went to help those who were not. The bandits put their blades away. Although the magic seized her neck so her head couldn't turn, she knew the dwarf was similarly affected, behind and to her left.

"I hope you're happy," she said. "There goes my fortune. Do you know how much that thing is worth?"

"Not really, no," he replied.

Damned no good dwarf. You'd think he'd be a li le more sympathetic toward a fellow vertically challenged individual trying to get by in a world of tall people.

The Eye weighed more than a quarter pound or so, solid gold. About a hundred gold pieces for the se ing. But she'd never seen a gem like that before — blue and green at the same time, with li le facets of red in *just* the right light. Nothing less than... a thousand — no — *two* thousand gold pieces.

"Three thousand gold pieces! Out the door. You absolute asshole."

"I can't hear you! Just hold on a minute, I can feel the magic moving off my head."

From behind Penellina came the sounds of furniture scraping, someone sobbing, another person swearing. Her eyes were fixed forward, past the broken door, giving her an unobstructed view of the kitchen. Inside, the innkeeper and his boy were taking their first furtive glances over the table tops.

The magic released her foot. As her toes hit the ground,

pins and needles shot up her leg. She whimpered and stomped. That seemed to liberate more of her. Before long the sickly warmth of the magic slipped off her. Once she was free, she knelt and checked her backpack, ge ing ready to leave. She wasn't about to let Josephus get away with her prize.

"Wait a moment," the dwarf said. "What's your name?"

He twisted lazily in the air, as though he dangled from an unseen fishing line — a puppet waiting for the puppet-master. Unlike the other dwarves she'd encountered, this one had an excessively groomed beard, plaited with li le beads throughout. He also wore a clean white shirt. His trousers seemed well-worn but equally well-mended. And those boots were the cleanest she'd seen on any traveller let alone on a dwarf.

"Penellina Dairgren," she said with a li le bow. "Master thief. And that" — she pointed in the vague direction of the kitchen — "was worth a kingdom."

"It was. I'm sorry I took it from you."

Her eyebrows shot up. "Well." She lowered them. "It was an asshole thing to do."

"You're right. But I need your help to get it back."

She laughed. "Why should I help you?"

"Because I need your help. You lifted that Eye from me without any trouble. And you've taken it from that big galoot before, if what he said is true."

Beyond the dwarf, more people shambled to their feet and rubbed their heads. Some left, throwing uncertain glances at the two of them. More than a few mu ered prayers under their breath at the sight of the magic at play. The bandits carried one of their compatriots out into the street. It could be useful to have an angry fighting dwarf

41

with her when she caught up to the Eye.

"Yes, well. What he says is not true."

"You didn't burgle him?"

She folded her arms. "No. I'm a thief, not a... not a burglar. Nor a robber. A burglar is unnecessarily destructive. A robber is aggressive. I'm neither of those things."

He lifted one eyebrow, glancing over the destruction.

"Besides, I didn't take it from him. He took it from me. We were... together. We broke up. It's my jewel. He stole it."

"I thought you said you mass-murdered a bunch of elv—" He looked at her in disbelief. "He's your lover?"

"Was."

"He's probably a paedophile."

A look of shock took over. "A rock spider? How do you figure?"

"Well, you're the size of a human child."

She held a finger to her chin. "That explains a lot. What do I get for helping you?"

"Gold."

"How much?"

"When we get the Eye back, and get it to my church in the mountains, say... four thousand."

She swallowed. "Four thousand *gold* pieces?" Not only was it enough to buy a kingdom, it was enough to pay for a few humans to help carry her things around. Plus she could always re-steal the Eye after she was paid. Infinite money...

With the tips of his boots now touching the ground, he tapped around to face her. "Yes. My church has more than enough money."

"Why should I believe you?"

"Because I can't tell any lies. Whurgan Ellagg forbids it."

42

"Whurgal Eel Lag?"

He smiled the eyeless smile of someone trying to sell her something she neither needed or wanted. "The god of dwarves. But not only dwarves, of all strong people. Do you have a god?"

"What's your name?"

"Farald."

She waited a moment. "Just 'Farald'? Don't you have a surname, like *Stoneblighter* or *Rockfingerer* or something?"

He raised his chin a li le. "No. I was stripped of my clan name."

She lowered her voice. "Shit. What did you do?"

His feet were flat on the ground now, but his arms still hung in the air. "I disobeyed my king. Among other things."

Penellina kept her face deep in thought while she pretended to mull over the offer. "Five thousand gold pieces and it's a deal."

"Deal."

After his arms came free, Farald moved about the room, straightening chairs and picking up broken crockery. Penellina studied him. Another of the wee people in the lands of big people, instinctively taking on his subservient role. And look! Here comes the angry taskmaster to tell him what he's doing wrong.

"You! I warned you! None of that... dwarven *shit*!" The innkeeper said, wielding a broom.

"It wasn't me," Farald said. "Ask her about it." He continued cleaning up.

The innkeeper stared at Penellina. His mouth opened and closed several times before he spoke again. "You're going to have to pay for all this," he declared.

"I didn't do anything!" Penellina whined. "All the

damage was caused by you big people!"

The innkeeper raised his broom and held it there. He was about to say something, but his shoulders slumped as the anger left his face. Le ing the broom fall, he went behind the bar and bent down into a cupboard. When he emerged, he wielded a glass bo le of thick, amber fluid. He started drinking.

"It won't be easy," Farald said over his shoulder to Penellina. "Not with that Vuhsi Kobold with him."

"Grilk? That's just his servant." She scrunched her nose. "I think it's a wizard."

"No. That's a Vuhsi Kobold. They don't come in 'servant'."

CHAPTER FOUR

The Road to Vuhsi

"GRILK, YOU ARE A TERRIBLE servant! I asked you to bring me the waterskin." Josephus watched his companion continue onward. "Would you stop for a moment?"

"Have Eye. Keep Eye."

Josephus sighed. "Grilk, please. We've gone way off the King's Trail, no one is going to find us out here."

The reptile hurried on toward Threerun, the golden Eye clutched in its claw. Josephus's boot squelched into another patch of mud.

"Grilk! I demand you stop. We need to rest."

A faint gradient of light bloomed beyond the low undulating hills in front of them. Remains of stunted trees, tufts of tall, coarse grass, and lichen covered, weather-rounded rocks do ed the rises. Josephus shivered and pulled his cloak tighter.

Grilk darted up a low, dead tree trunk and surveyed the area ahead. It waited for Josephus, then dropped the waterskin to the ground when he caught up.

45

"You rest." Grilk looked over the surroundings. "I no need."

"Fine. That's fine. Are you at least hungry?"

"Yes. I find."

Josephus shuddered at the thought of eating one of Grilk's 'found' meals. "I've got some rations here, dried potatoes and peas... a bit of pork I think. Get some kindling, would you?"

The reptile's yellow eyes stared down at him.

"We need a fire to cook the potatoes and peas," Josephus explained. "I've told you before. You must cook your food."

It skittered off into the mud and rocks without another word. Josephus gave the tree a little kick. The timber felt dry enough. He pulled at it but managed to splinter off only an arm-sized chunk. Enough for now. He'd send Grilk out for some more, but not before he'd given his companion some time to drive the chill from its bones.

Resting on a somewhat smooth stone, Josephus prepared their meal — filling a pot with water from the skin, dropping the dried food in. He sat the two wooden bowls and spoons close by, as well as the matching cups. This wasn't exactly what the hero should be doing, at least not according to the legends. No — one of his followers should be preparing the meal, while another regaled him with a story. Perhaps one would be secretly in love with him — an unrequited love of course — unable to announce her thoughts out of misguided fear of his gravitas.

It was a shame Penny betrayed him so quickly. A lesson learned. *Not everyone I meet will be an ally*, he thought. *And as we get closer to the end, the antagonists will get more dangerous.*

Grilk returned with a few sticks bundled up in its arms and dumped them in front of Josephus. They were wet, and more than a few looked as though it'd just dug them out of the mud.

"Really, Grilk." Josephus tried to keep patient with his unlearned friend. "They are to be *dry* if we're to have a fire."

The lizard said something in its indecipherable tongue and flicked a spark at the pile. A fire licked up through the twigs, popping and crackling. Josephus paused and frowned before he pulled his log over the top. He placed the flint and steel back into his pack, then began to cook.

From within its cloak, Grilk retrieved a handful of what appeared to be maggots. Josephus groaned and looked away as it brought down its snout and licked them up. It chewed, snapping its long jaw together, bits of white grub bursting.

"Grilk, will you please chew with your mouth closed?"

It peered at him, cocking its head to the side. "No lips."

Josephus nodded in acquiescence — it was a conversation they'd had before. Shaking his head, he stirred the pot, adding a pinch of salt. He shifted his weight on the rock. It had been a long night.

"You seem quiet, Grilk. What's on your mind?"

"Time."

"Oh? You think we're running out of time?"

"Yes. Evil comes."

"I know the prophecy well. We have plenty of time to return to Threerun and get the next instructions from Master Thornton."

Grilk's tail swished behind him. "Thornton bad."

"What?" Josephus glanced up from his stirring.

"Thornton bad. Not help. Delay. Greedy."

Josephus sighed and shook his head again. His li le companion knew nothing of the world of civilised man. *It must all seem very confusing,* he thought.

47

"No, no. Master Thornton is our friend. Each artefact we've brought him will help us defeat the evil."

They sat in silence as the pot came to a boil. When the taste was to Josephus's satisfaction, he filled the two bowls and handed one to Grilk. The reptile sniffed at it and took a few tentative bites.

"Grilk." Josephus held up his spoon. "Use your spoon."

The reptile did as he instructed, mimicking the movements of an educated creature. He wondered if he could ever bring his companion out of its ignorance.

The fire swept up over the log.

"Tell me. Why have you never lit the fire before? I didn't know you were capable of that spell."

Grilk sat the spoon down into its half-finished meal. "No ask."

"I didn't know you could freeze people like that either. Or make them levitate." Josephus looked up in thought. "What other spells do you know?"

"Many."

"How many?"

Its claw disappeared into its cloak and retrieved a small book. It was bound in thick, uneven leather, the pages made of crude parchment. The whole thing looked as though it had been soaked through and dried many times. Josephus had seen it before, when he first met Grilk, but assumed it to be just another piece of junk it insisted on carting around.

"Spells," Grilk said, handing the book to Josephus.

He opened it. The pages crackled in reluctance as he turned them. Tiny claw marks — short, sharp lines punctuated by dots — covered each sheet. If it was writing, it was disorganised. Some of the lines curved as they ran along, others were vertical rather than horizontal. A few lines squeezed into the spaces between other lines, changing size to fit.

In his teenage years, Josephus spent some time under the tutelage of magical scholars — though he never developed the knack for it. As such, he knew the eccentricities of the learned magic users, of the uniqueness of an individual's spell-book.

"Grilk, I had no idea you were a wizard."

The lizard studied him with the same tilt of its head. "I magic, all the time."

"Yes, yes. But I had assumed it was some innate... sorcery. Or at best some tribal magic from a lesser god. Illiterate. This is really quite something. I must remember to tell Master Thornton about this."

"No!" Grilk snatched the book and hid it within the folds of its cloak. "No tell Thornton."

"I told you, Grilk. We can trust him. You must understand who your be   ers are."

The tail curled up its side. "I no trust. You no tell or I no magic."

Josephus stared into Grilk's yellow eyes. He leaned forward. "We have been through a lot together. And although you are uncivilized, bad mannered, and don't seem to know your place — I consider you a friend. I will say nothing of your magic to Master Thornton."

While it annoyed Josephus that Grilk had the audacity to assume the Chosen One needed its magic, he was also a magnanimous leader. Satisfying the li le thing harmed no one.

The reptile nodded. "Rest now. Two hours."

"That's fine, Grilk." Josephus wondered if he'd find more companions to join him on his quest. Maybe ones who weren't so odd. "Will you keep watch?"

"I lookout."

"You're not tired?"

Grilk folded his arms and raised his snout slightly. "I no need sleep."

FARALD LOOKED UP AT THE morning sky and gave a prayer of thanks to Whurgan Ellagg. Penellina was a decent tracker — she found the marks in the mud where their quarry left the road — but it must have been the invisible hand of his god that guided them over the hills. It hadn't taken them much to catch up to the Eye. The blond man — 'Josephus', she'd informed him — and the Vuhsi were asleep in the open.

The flap of Josephus's backpack was open, exposing The Eye within.

"You sure you want me to wait all the way back here?" Farald asked.

"Yes. You're noisy. Your armour ra les when you walk, and you even breathe hard when you eat," Penellina said. "Any closer and they'll hear you."

Farald studied his breastplate. "I suppose even if they wake up, he won't hurt you."

Penellina looked up from tightening the laces on her boots. "Why do you say that?"

"Well… I'm sure there's still some affection between you two. At least on his part; a man can't just discard his feelings that easily," Farald said, then mu ered, "Even if they're for a woman the size of a child."

"I'm twenty-five," Penellina said, puffing up her chest in righteousness. "And why are you calling me li le? You're not much bigger than me!"

"Okay, okay." He gestured for Penellina to calm down

and stay quiet. "All I'm trying to say is that he probably won't hurt you if he catches you. Until recently, he did love you."

"Oh right." She broke her eyes away. "I'll level with you. That was a lie."

He cocked his head. "What else was a lie?"

She looked off to the side in thought for a moment. "Just that. I think."

The halfling set out in li le bursts of activity, ducking behind a larger stone or clump of thicker grass. Farald kept his own head down, peering through a gap in the branches of a gnarled bush.

When she had crossed half the distance, she turned and gave him a thumbs up, a big cheeky grin stretched across her face. He returned it, nodding. "Go on, go on," he urged under his breath. Though Farald didn't relish the idea of theft, she definitely seemed to be enjoying herself. He was sure Whurgan would forgive him this sin. The Eye was far too powerful to be left to a Vuhsi.

As she got closer, Josephus stirred and rolled in his blanket. Farald gripped his war hammer and stood, se   ing his feet ready for a charge. As he did, he knocked the hammer's handle against his armour, the clank was overly loud. Penellina mouthed something with an 'F' and shooed him away. He paused a moment before complying — she wouldn't be able to fight them alone.

Josephus's stirring ceased, and from even this distance, his snores could be heard. Farald spared a glance for the Vuhsi, but it still looked as dead as when they arrived — cloak covering its head, laying on its back, sprawled over a stone. Its snout rested open and to the side. It looked so exposed and powerless.

51

Of course it wasn't dead or helpless. At best it was as asleep as the man it kept as a pet. At worst it was a ruse. Farald tried to warn Penellina, but she was convinced there was no danger.

"Look at it," she had said. "It's tired from all the magic. That's what my grandmother used to tell me, that sorcerers and whatnot get tired after using magic."

Farald tried to explain the difference between the various magical forms — not all make you tired — but her eyes glazed as soon as he started. He'd had students like her. They never made it far in school, they had to see or do for themselves for the lesson to stick. Tightening his grip on the war hammer, he gauged the distance between him and the Vuhsi, hoping this wouldn't be one of those lessons.

She moved around the final bush, beyond which was a twenty yard stretch before she could reach the backpack. Penellina timed each step forward with one of Josephus's snores. The slow pace was agonizing. Farald wouldn't be able to get to her in time if something went wrong. Guilt pulled at him, and he feared Whurgan Ellagg would once again judge him lacking. He hung his head a moment.

When Farald looked up, she was on her way back to him, a smile on her face, the Eye no longer in the backpack. She held a hand over her smiling mouth, suppressing a giggle. When she got back to the last bush, she took a different route along the base of the low mound Josephus and the Vuhsi camped beside. She got down on her belly and crawled along. It was a more circuitous path, but the low rise would hide her from view.

After mouthing a thank you to the clouds above, he lowered his eyes to keep a watch on the two sleepers.

When she was three quarters of the way back, she

52

stopped, her face quizzical. She picked up what looked to be a small branch and held it to her ear. *What in the hells is she doing?*

After a moment, Penellina pulled her head back in surprise and turned the stick about, investigating it. She shrugged, shook her head, and tossed the stick.

As it sailed through the air, a red split blossomed along its length. It opened wide, revealing a mouth — complete with teeth and tongue — and called out. The voice boomed, as though it were a skilled dwarven baritone. "ALARM! ALARM! ALARM!"

The Vuhsi reacted instantly, pulling its cloak together and darting over to Josephus. It grabbed his bedroll and shook him, shouting in its foul language. Josephus grumbled at first, trying to swat the kobold away, but a slap across the face brought him rising. The Vuhsi said something Farald couldn't hear, then the man grabbed his sword.

Penellina stayed low and raced along the ground, increasing the distance between her and the tell-tale stick. She was still hidden from Josephus and Grilk by the low rise. They stalked toward her position, the Vuhsi pointing in one direction while stepping in the other.

Farald held his war hammer down and to the side and rushed forward. Surprised by his own speed, he closed the gap quickly. The cla er and crash of his armour focused the Vuhsi's a ention on him. Farald bellowed his god's name, and surged forward.

Penellina stood and ran away from all three of them. The split-second distraction was enough for Farald to swing his hammer and catch the Vuhsi unaware. His foot found soft mud, disrupting the angle of the swing. The broadside of the hammer struck the kobold's abdomen, hurtling it through

53

the air.

Josephus cried out and drove his blade toward Farald. Farald glanced the a ack aside with the shaft of his weapon. He ignored Josephus, stepped forward and pressed the kobold. He readied his hammer for an overhead swing.

As Farald's hammer came down, Josephus tackled him. The weight of the man drove Farald down, losing his grip on his weapon. With one hand, he punched at Josephus, with the other he groped for the reassurance of the war hammer's thick wooden handle.

Farald spared a glance for the Vuhsi as it got to its feet. Abandoning his steel, Farald renewed his struggle, hi ing Josephus as hard and quick as he could. A rock bounced off Josephus's head. His eyes rolled back and he fell to the side.

Farald tackled the kobold and grabbed at its arms, trying to pin it down. He thought he had it, but its wiry arms pulled free. All of a sudden it wasn't there, only an empty cloak on the ground. A claw pressed into the side of Farald's neck as another gripped the back of his head.

"Give up. Or dead." Its voice was like stone and wood grinding together.

Farald dropped his shoulders and raised his hands. "I should warn you now, Vuhsi. I've killed your kind before."

It made a sound like a laugh, then jerked him around.

"Let him go, or I kill your master!"

Penellina stood over the unconscious Josephus, her dagger against his throat. The claw in Farald's neck relented a li le.

"I mean it! I'll fuckin' kill him I swear!" Her voice was shrill.

The lizard made no movement or sound. She dragged the blade a half-inch, a thin red line appeared beneath it.

54

Her voice lost its edge. "Don't make me."

Farald felt the Vuhsi shove him forward. He took the few steps to Penellina and mouthed a thank you before turning. The creature's skin was reptilian — grey that faded to browns and greens. Small horns broke through in irregular pa erns. Leather pouches and belts criss-crossed the lizard's body, arms, and legs; only the tail remained unadorned. Few of the pockets were the same size or even appeared to be the same age.

"What want?"

"To keep the Eye from the likes of you," Farald said.

"Yeah. Fuck off you pet-sized dragon!"

"No. Need Eye. Need man."

Farald looked down at Josephus's prone body. "If *you* want him, he's be er off dead."

Penellina looked up at him, scared. "I don't want to kill him," she whispered. "Not really."

Farald shook his head. "This man is as good as dead. That Vuhsi is luring him for some dark ritual, why else would they be so far off the road?"

Her eyes widened. "Maybe it was looking for a quiet place to kill him?"

"No kill. Prophecies. Bad things happen."

Farald looked back to the Vuhsi. "Prophecy? Which one?" Nothing good ever came from prophecies.

"Azair Soloth."

That's right, Josephus had mentioned Azair Soloth at the inn. It was generally considered only a minor prophecy, and though it spoke of evil, it wasn't considered a world-destroying evil. "*You're* helping him quell the evil that rises in these lands?"

"Yes. And Loexkear Irthir'erekess."

55

Farald narrowed his eyes. "Both prophecies are still active?"

The Vuhsi nodded, its yellow eyes fixed on Farald's.

Farald hesitated, then reached down and eased Penellina's knife away from Josephus's throat. "Let's check that bump on his noggin." His voice became grim. "We wouldn't want the world to end."

PENELLINA SAT IN THE LATE morning sun, using her teeth to pull at a piece of dried chicken. It made her jaw hurt as she chewed it, but she was too hungry to care. She flashed a smile at Grilk as it handed her back the Eye. She looked at both Farald and the lizard. "So...," she said around the mass of masticated meat. "You say there are two prophecies that have the Eye?"

"That's right," Farald said. He dabbed a wet cloth against the cut on the side of Josephus's still unconscious head.

"And they're opposites?"

"Not exactly 'opposite', but they do conflict with each other. To be fulfilled, they both require the Eye of Aera. But fulfilment of either one would consume the magic confined within the Eye. So only one of them can come true."

Penellina held a finger against her lip and looked up at the morning sky, recalling everything her grandfather had told her about prophecies and prophets. He wasn't a fan. "Am I in a prophecy? We're all here, so surely the stoners foresaw — forsoothed? — *foreseened* we'd be a part of it?" She looked expectantly at the two of them.

Farald shook his head. "The use of hallucinogens by prophets is purely functional. One does not simply *have* visions of the future. Sometimes they require a li le chemical help, but that hardly makes them 'stoners'."

"What, like… 'functional addicts' then?"

"No. No others in Loex." Grilk had pulled its hood down low over its eyes. Its tail drew a casual pa   ern in the drying mud.

"Azair doesn't mention anyone else that I remember. The prophecies aren't happening exactly as foretold," Farald said. "That could be a problem."

Penellina turned the Eye around in her hand, projecting prismatic colours against the ground. It was so *pre   y*. Maybe she could take it awa—

"—Careful. The old magic in these things tends to corrupt mortals."

She frowned and stuffed it into Josephus's bag. "Wait. Why is it a problem that we've not been foreseened?"

"Because it means somewhere, something or someone has changed things. The prophecies are no longer… prophetic."

"Prophetic? I don't think that's a word, it doesn't sound right. Anyway this doesn't make sense, how can a prophecy not be prophetical anymore?"

"Think of it this way. There are what?" Farald looked at Grilk. "Hundreds? Thousands of prophecies?"

The lizard nodded.

"Most of them are a vision of one possible future. Usually they involve an event at a nexus point."

"Nexus?"

"Every decision is a split in the road of time, you go left or right. *Every* decision. A nexus point is where some of those different roads come back together. Prophecies involve those events. If decisions before it happen differently, the event changes."

The words came in the familiar drone of someone who's recited them countless times to bored students. Penellina had a knack for knowing when a lecture was coming. She rolled her eyes. "So? Who cares?"

"These two prophecies are unique in that they involve a Chosen One."

Penellina brightened, she knew the answer to this one. "That's Josephus! He's the chosen one!"

"Yes. Both prophecies claim the Chosen One will make their predictions come true. Prophecies with Chosen Ones are more like guarantees than predictions."

Her mouth curved to the side in thought. "But... they can't both be true?"

"No. And the big problem is, we're only a few days away from the nexus. At least in my understanding of the Azair Soloth prophecy." He scratched the side of his face. "The Chosen One will quell the evil that rises in the lands," he intoned thoughtfully. He looked at Grilk for confirmation.

The lizard nodded. "Yes, and Loex prophecy soon."

"So they shouldn't both still be active. One should have fallen to the wayside days, even weeks ago. At least that's usually how these things go."

Penellina stood and flexed her legs. They'd been si ing around talking for too long. "Who cares? It doesn't involve us, you said so yourself. We could sell the Eye for five thousand gold pieces" — she counted off her fingers — "that's twelve hundred each." She clenched her fist in victory. "And a li le extra for me."

"I'm afraid it does involve us now. We've got everything an important prophecy needs. A wizard, a thief, a warrior, a priest. The gods have a certain... *style* when it comes to prophesied quests and whatnot."

Penellina kicked a stone and harrumphed. "Fuck this noise. I want my gold."

"Greedy. Bad."

"I've got to agree with the Vuhsi."

Penellina rolled her eyes. "A minute ago you were trying to kill it."

"That was before it spoke of the Loexkear Irthir'erekess prophecy — am I saying that right?"

Grilk waved its hand in a so-so motion.

Penellina practised a cartwheel. "When we sell the Eye, I'm going to buy an invisible cloak and steal some magic stuff from a wizarding school."

Farald threw his hands up in frustration, performing a fantastic imitation of her school teachers after she'd decided she'd learned enough for the day.

Penellina groaned. "I don't understand why this is so important. They can't both be true, right? So just one of them happens and we sell the Eye."

"It's important because when two prophecies compete right up to the nexus point... weird shit happens. We're talking 'end of an age' kind of events here, the ones that break a spoke on the wheel of time."

Penellina flopped to the ground and crossed her legs. Everyone was silent for a moment. She frowned at the prone Josephus. "He's the chosen one in both prophecies?"

Farald nodded. "I'm not sure how, but it appears he is. The Vuhsi's chief believes him to be their Chosen One."

"And he *thinks* he's completing the Azair prophecy?"

"That's what he said. The Vuhsi here says the same thing."

"But you" — she pointed at Grilk — "are trying to complete the lizardy prophecy?"

59

Grilk's snout bobbed up and down.

"Why were you doing that?"

Farald held his hand out at Grilk. "Because the Loex prophecy tells of a man who brings forth the Vuhsi god." He looked at Grilk. "Is that about right?"

"Yes. How know?"

"I've had cause to learn from the kobold mystics." Farald turned away. "Many years ago."

Grilk tilted its head to the side, then continued. "But, I learn two prophecy. Bad like you say. I stop both prophecy, then no bad."

Farald leaned his chin against his hand. "That's a dangerous game, Vuhsi. The gods don't like it when we meddle."

"Best choice. Stop bad."

"Of course," Farald said. "If it can be done, it solves everything."

"What solves what?" Penellina asked.

"Grilk has been aiding Josephus to complete the Azair prophecy while also completing the Loex prophecy. If we string the prophecies along until the last moment, we can sever them both. Then neither comes true."

"...but if neither happens... what about the fork in the road?"

"Existence just replaces it with a straight road. No big event that sunders the earth in twain." Farald leaned his head back to see the sky. "I think. There are a couple stories about it happening before."

"Can't we just melt the Eye down? Sell the gem, sell the gold?"

"We couldn't harm it unless we had some kind of magical weapon. Something even more powerful than the

Eye."

"So… what now?"

Farald looked at Grilk. "We continue with the Vuhsi's plan. Lead Josephus along the path to complete both prophecies, then stop him."

"Go Threerun. Thornton give next step. He have book of prophecy."

"Okay," Farald said. "There should still be a Whurgan Ellagg church in the city. I can get some help there."

"And after we're done screwing around with fate we sell the Eye?" Penellina asked.

"Yes," Farald said.

"Great! Count me in."

Farald chuckled. "You couldn't count yourself out at this point. You've been swept up into this whether you like it or not."

They sat in silence. Penellina grew concerned. Who would they sell the Eye to? She didn't know anyone who had six thousand gold pieces. Maybe it would be be er to take it back to her village; her grandfather or grandmother might know of a decent fence. She'd pay these guys back eventually. Probably. If she saw them again.

Josephus groaned and stirred as Farald cleaned the cut on his neck. The man's eyes flu ered.

"Grilk?"

"Yes. Here."

"Why is the dwarf here?"

"Friend now. Help prophecy."

With Farald and Grilk's help, Josephus sat upright. His eyes fell on Penellina.

"Grilk?

"Yes?"

"Why is the halfling here?"

"Friend now. Help prophecy."

Josephus touched the side of his head and checked the ends of his fingers. "Did something hit me in the head?"

"Halfling, slingshot. Why you no duck?"

"I haven't got eyes in the back of my head, Grilk." Josephus paused a moment before shaking his head. "Penny. That was a good shot. You've a great eye." He rubbed the side of his face as he scanned around them. "Well. Prophecy awaits friends. We should get a move on."

His smile was contagious. Penellina smiled back and handed his bag to him. When no one spoke, she pulled Farald aside.

"Do you think he's alright?"

Farald shrugged. "You gave him a good whack. I don't know." He shrugged again. "Who knows? humans, right?"

"Are we going to tell him the plan?"

Farald threw a conspiratorial arm around her shoulders and pulled her in close. "No," he murmured. "He's the Chosen One in *both* prophecies. If we tell him, he might do something wrong and then we won't know what's happening."

"So we're going to lie to the Chosen One?"

"No, *I'm* not. *You* are. If he asks any questions, you answer for me."

Penellina folder her arms. "That's the stupidest thing I've ever heard."

"I told you before, I *can't* lie. Whurgan Ellagg forbids it. The best I can do is not tell the truth."

This could be fun. "Am I the best thief you've ever met?"

Farald pulled a pained face. It took a moment for him to respond. "You're my second favourite thief."

Penellina laughed quietly. "Nice cover. But can't we just stop him now? Then neither comes true?"

"If we don't wait until the last moment, something will come up and fill the void to try and complete the prophecies. Things always culminate at a nexus."

"Is everyone ready?" Josephus sounded well-rested and confident.

There wasn't much between his ears, but ge ing up so easily after being unconscious was a li   le disconcerting. And he didn't seem at all fazed that she and Farald were now on his side.

"I hope he's alright," she said, more to herself than anyone else.

"I hope so too," Farald answered. "Right now, he's the most important person in the world."

CHAPTER FIVE

Threerun

FARALD YAWNED AND RUBBED AT his eyes as he gazed up at the wooden palisade that surrounded Threerun. It was twelve feet high and solidly built — not bad work for humans. Traffic on the road had come to a stop, and he volunteered to go on ahead and find out what was going on.

Threerun was centred at a junction of three of the King's Trails. Over the years he'd known it, it had grown from a well-known campground for merchants into the bustling city it was today. And still it was growing. Proper constructions were beginning to replace the common shanty towns that mound and grow up against city walls. Cooking smoke and animal scents drifted over the road and between the buildings. The path was full of people, farmers, merchants — common folk, all human — vying to get through the closed timber gates.

With a few pardons and apologies, Farald emerged from the mass of people to find a lone guard facing the street. He wore simple armour, with a red sash that flowed from the right pauldron to his belt, but no weapon. The guard stood with his arms crossed and tight lips raised at one corner. The people left a ten foot space around him. He looked down his nose as Farald approached.

"What's the hold-up, mate?" Farald asked.

"The west gate is closed for the morning," the guard said with an exaggerated sigh. "It'll be open in a couple hours."

"Why's the gate closed?"

"Does it ma er? Piss off."

Farald grumbled his way back to his new companions, all leaning against the low stonework of a recently built tavern. In times past, the wall would have been extended to provide safety for these new additions to the city, but humans weren't what they used to be. Two unarmed bouncers stood to either side of the wide, welcoming doors. One of them scowled as Farald approached. Farald ignored him and considered the people he now kept company with.

Josephus leaned with one ankle crossed over the over, working dirt out from under his fingernails. The Vuhsi hunched down, drawing himself into the darkness of its cloak. Penellina tossed a dagger up in the air above her head and watched it strike the ground, she pulled it out from the dirt.

"Hey! So what's the verdict?" she asked.

"Gate's closed. It'll be open in a couple hours."

"Why's it closed?" she asked.

"They won't say."

"Probably clearing out the slums again," Josephus said. "The criminals can't run away if they seal up the city."

Penellina laughed. "You're kidding right?"

"There's a lot of criminals in Threerun, Penny," Josephus said. "As you know."

65

"Why would I know?" Penellina held her dagger up with lazy menace. "Just what is it that you're implying?"

"I'm not making any implications," Josephus said, rubbing some of the fingernail muck with his thumb. "I just assumed that seeing as you're... well, seeing as you live in the, should we say, 'lower-class areas', I figured you know how dangerous it can be."

"Right! Yes." She sheathed her dagger. "It is dangerous. Sometimes, we all have to do what we can to survive. You know?"

Josephus closed his eyes and nodded. "I'm sorry you and your friends have had to live that way. I'm sure it's not easy. If not for their circumstances, I'm sure they would have done more to find you."

"Don't worry about it," Penellina said with a smile. "So, what's the plan?"

Farald squinted one eye at Josephus before continuing. Was he oblivious to her lies? Penellina was right, that rock to the head may have done some permanent damage. "We'll go talk to this Master Thornton, find out what the next step is."

"Right, where's he live?" she asked.

Josephus waved his hand toward the city. "He lives on the south eyot, right on top of the hill."

Penellina scrunched her nose. "The south *what*?"

Josephus rolled his eyes. "The south *island*."

"Oh right yeah, of course, the eeyachts."

As the two continued talking, Farald glanced down at the Vuhsi. It had remained silent throughout the overnight journey. What he wouldn't give to know what the thing was thinking.

"Right," Farald interrupted them. "Can't we go around to one of the other gates?"

Both he and Penellina looked up at Josephus.

"The north and east gates? But we'd have to get a ferry across the river. In any case, if they're clearing the slums, the others would be just as closed as this—"

A bell tolled from within the city as urgent voices rose up all around. From behind the wall, someone shouted up at the palisade walkways. The guards along the barrier bellowed down at the road, ordering people to make way for the gates. The crowd backed away, retreating to their carts or homes.

The gates burst open. A stream of people rushed out — humans, elves, a dwarf or two. There were even more than a few orcish faces, and Farald was sure he saw a gnome before it disappeared around a shack. They instantly milled through the waiting carts and travellers, causing chaos, with everyone trying to get to their destination simultaneously.

A fleeing dwarf fell into a culvert on the side of the road. Farald weaved his way through the throng and found the dwarf struggling to extricate himself from the mud. Holding onto a fence post and stepping down, Farald reached his hand out.

"Here, take my hand," he said.

The dwarf thrashed his arm at Farald. "I'm fine, I'm fine. I can manage myself, you damned runt." He fell on his backside.

"Don't be stubborn, I'm here to help."

The dwarf stood and swayed. His beard was untidy, his clothes a shambles. Sourness twisted his face into a grimace. "Piss off."

Farald let his hand fall then returned to his companions. Penellina watched him struggle to cross the street, her brow drawn down over her eyes. Josephus and the Vuhsi remained as they were.

"What was that about?" Penellina asked with a smirk. "You don't get along with other dwarves?"

Farald avoided her eyes. "He's drunk. Doesn't know what he's doing."

"That's a surprise," Josephus chuckled.

Farald looked back at the dwarf, still trying to climb out. "It's not his fault," he said. "They lack structure here. A dwarf needs structure."

"They've only ever told me they need alms," Josephus said. "Or booze."

The Vuhsi made a sound like a short laugh.

Farald hung his head; they were right. Most of the dwarves found outside the mountain homes were exiles, criminals, or outcasts. He watched the dwarf finally step back onto the road and gaze around at the busy street. They locked eyes.

"You leave ol' Dwon alone, you bloody prick!" the dwarf yelled at Farald. "I'm not like you. I'm a *real* dwarf. I don't need no damn help from no damned piss-ant."

Josephus stifled a laugh. Farald showed the dwarf his back.

After a minute, the people thinned out, leaving the gate open.

"I guess we can go in now," Farald said. "Come on."

A disorderly queue began to coalesce in front of a lone guard standing in the gateway. The man licked a thumb and flicked through a stack of parchment sheets handed to him by a very patient merchant. Farald steered them around the line.

As they crossed the threshold, the guard challenged them. "Halt! You must present for inspection!"

Farald stepped up to the guard and squared his shoulders. Humans always looked down on his people. It angered him. But what was worse was that they had just cause. They only knew of the drunken dwarf. The surly, bi er li le being that lashed out at the freedom of the world outside the mountain homes. Annoyed with the guard's earlier treatment of him, Farald stared up and snarled. "Piss off!"

He shouldered his way past. Other people waiting to get in decided to circumvent proper procedure as well. The guard spu ered indignation.

The road was packed with people, making progress slow. Farald kept to the main cobblestone thoroughfare until they reached a fork in the road. Up the hill to the north were the temples and churches, the area he was most familiar with. To the east the road crossed to the southern island before crossing again into the rest of the city.

Farald stopped and addressed his companions. "Let's split up here," he said. "Penellina, you go with Josephus to Thornton. The Vuhsi and I will head up the hill, to the Whurgan Ellagg church here."

"Wait. Why?" Josephus asked. "What does Grilk need with a dwarf god? And why do you keep calling Grilk that?"

"I'm calling it what it is, and I want to find out a li le more about this prophecy of yours. You know, to help you." Farald was a li le surprised to find he could bend the truth that far, but he supposed it technically wasn't a lie.

"I go. I Take Eye."

Josephus looked at the Vuhsi. "This makes no sense. Come, Grilk." He regarded Farald and Penellina. "You two can both come along as well."

"No," the Vuhsi said. "You go. I Take Eye. I go church.

Be er. Trust Grilk."

Josephus paused a moment before agreeing. "Okay Grilk. I trust you. Come along Penny, I'll introduce you to Master Thornton. He's really very charming. Keep on your guard, he's even more disarming than me."

Penellina jogged to catch up with Josephus's sure stride.

Grilk was looking at Farald. "Thornton bad."

"How so?"

"Greedy. Sell Eye. Sell artefacts."

"What's his interest in the prophecy?"

"More artefacts. More money."

Farald frowned. "Let's go up to my church. I need to converse with god."

PENELLINA SQUIRMED AND KICKED HER foot out of Josephus's hands. He was vigorously running a cloth over her boots.

"Please keep still, Penny. It'll only be a few more minutes."

"I don't see what it ma ers," she said. "It's just dirt."

"You're not in the squalor of the slums anymore, Penny. People here don't appreciate wayward adventurers trailing mud across their floors."

She relented and tapped her hands on the barrel. They sat outside Master Thornton's residence, a stone and timber tower that appeared taller than it truly was. It sat upon the pinnacle of a steep hill that ju ed out from the current of the wide river — cleverly named *Threerun River* — that split the city in two, giving it additional artificial height. A road carved its way around the hill. Each residence was placed spaciously in the centre of a large plot, making use of the natural stone and shape of the land. A touch of elven influence in their positioning. Each driveway had its own

70

ornate entrance with li le bits of stonework, trimmed shrubbery, or elaborately designed, wrought iron fences.

Like subjects beneath their ruler, the estates surrounded the tower, which unlike the other buildings, had no wall. Instead, it occupied the top of a plateau, stone cliffs providing a natural barrier to entry. Large trees spo ed the top of the ridge, their roots plunging down the rock face to the soil below. Their foliage speckled light shadow over the island.

It was all so unfamiliar to her, completely unlike the low, semi-underground dwellings of her village, or the utilitarian buildings she'd seen in the few human towns and hamlets she'd visited. She could feel the sense of proud pompousness emanating from the surroundings. Bunch of assholes. You didn't make it to somewhere like this without stepping on a few of the li le people.

"So this Thornton guy," she said. "He's like, what? Your... boss?"

He replied without looking up from her feet. "In a way, I suppose he is. He took me in when I was young. Trained me."

In her clan, everyone raised everyone's kids, but she'd heard of the rigidity of family connections among men. "Oh, so he's your wealthy uncle?"

It took a moment for Josephus to reply. "No. I'm adopted."

Oh, this was interesting! "He's your... father?"

"In a way. But, no. He's more like my *teacher*."

"Oh I get it. I was close to my teacher too. Except he was *also* my grandfather."

"Does he still live here?"

She looked off to the side. "No. I moved here a while ago. He's still back in my village."

Josephus nodded his understanding. "A rural girl? It

71

must be fate that set you on a path to me. Bards will tell grand stories of us. There we go."

Penellina looked down at her boots. She wasn't completely sure what he had done, they looked as brown as they ever did. "If you're satisfied, can we go in now?"

"Of course." Josephus stood and led the way to the front doors. They were ten feet tall, polished oak, with a li le iron-barred window at human height that was currently closed. He knocked loudly on the door.

When they first stepped off the road on the island, she expected such obviously wealthy people to be more security conscious. But this tower, and as near as she could tell the houses too, lay completely open. There were ample avenues for ingress and egress, and so far she hadn't seen any guards.

"Josephus, is Master Thornton a wizard?"

"What?" He looked down at her. "No. Whatever gave you that idea?"

She made a mental note to return to the island tonight.

Footfalls heralded the opening of the door. She stepped back as it swung outward. A frowning woman appeared. She was slender, a li le shorter than Josephus. Her eyes and ears betrayed her obvious elven heritage, but Penellina knew a half-breed when she saw one.

"Yes?" the woman asked. "What do you want?"

"Tho," Josephus smiled and opened his arms wide. "It's me!"

"Name?"

He dropped his arms and groaned. "Josephus of Threerun."

Her eyes were blank as she waited.

"Here for an audience with Master Thornton." He waited a moment. "Come on, Tho. Let me in."

She opened the door wider and beckoned him in. Penellina followed and smiled up at the half-elf.

The entire base of the tower was a single circular room. Ten feet above, thick beams of dark wood crossed the ceiling. Several chandeliers hung from the beams, though none were lit — all of the light came from wide windows high up the walls. Josephus and Tho's feet echoed on the flat stone floor. Penellina kept hers from doing so.

On one side of the room were rows of shelves. From this angle, Penellina couldn't see all of them, but what she did see looked expensive. Some held books while others twinkled with hints of gold and gemstones. One night sneaking around in here could set her up for life.

She tugged on Josephus's shirt. "Is that Tho lady a wizard?"

"No. Why do you keep asking about wizards?"

"Well…" Penellina thought a moment before risking the question. "There's a lot of stuff here. Aren't you all afraid of burglars?"

"Oh," he laughed. "No. We're all paid up with the th—"

"—Josephus! You've returned!" Master Thornton's voice was deep and confident. It had a jovial undercurrent as though everything was accompanied with a chuckle. "Do you have it? Do you have the *Eye*?"

He descended the wide stone stairs that hugged the wall in front of them. His ample frame was clothed in a dark red robe, close to black, with gold brocades running over the hemlines. She wouldn't call him fat, but he definitely looked like he was aging with contentment. His long dark hair bundled up around his shoulders. She smelled perfume with his arrival.

"Yes, I have the Eye," Josephus confirmed.

"Well" — Thornton held his hands out — "let's get a look at it." His eyes glistened with the kind of greed Penellina rarely saw even in herself.

"I don't have it with me."

"You what?" He lowered his brow. "Then where, pray tell, is it?"

"Grilk has it."

"Grilk? Oh right, the kobold. Why does Grilk have it?" He chuckled a li le, as though it were an afterthought.

Penellina interrupted. "Josephus thought it would be best."

"I di—?"

She kicked his shin, keeping a smile plastered on her face. "Keep it safe from thieves," she said as a ma er of fact.

Thornton thought for a moment before a wide smile bloomed across his face. He nodded. "Good thinking. Good thinking, Josephus. But you must remember to bring it back soon. Tell me, who's your friend?"

"May I introduce Penellina Dairgren. A companion I've picked up on my travels."

"Another one? At least she looks respectable." He looked Penellina up and down. "Somewhat."

"Don't let her diminutive stature fool you, father. She's quite the li le warrior, in fact she saved me from—"

"—Don't call me that. I'm not your father. Your father abandoned you to the street. If your mother even knew who he was," His voice momentarily lost its frivolous tone.

Josephus hung his head. "Sorry, master."

This Thornton fellow annoyed Penellina. Josephus may be an arrogant dickhead, but he didn't deserve that bullshit.

"You have another quest," Thornton said.

Josephus smiled weakly. "Another quest, master. Where

74

to this time?"

"You're almost done. You are indeed the Chosen One." He put his arm around Josephus and led them both toward a small dining table. When the three sat down, Thornton clapped his hands. Tho left the room.

"The first thing you need to do is bring the Eye here."

"Won't I need it for the quest, master? The prophecy does say something about needing it on a final quest."

"Yes, yes of course. It does, yes..." He looked up at Penellina. "But listen to us talking of work. Tell me, Penellina, what is it that you do?"

"I'm a... scribe, very boring. You know," she added quickly. "Josephus has told me so much about you."

Thornton sat upright and smiled, his eyebrows raised in expectation.

"Yeah, he told me you were a man of impeccable taste. Quite the — 'connoisseur' was the word he used — of rare and beautiful artefacts." She drew a pa   ern on the table with her finger. "I was kind of hoping that you might show me some."

Josephus looked confused but another tap with her foot kept him quiet.

"Of course! Come, come," Thornton said as he rose from the table.

Penellina followed, leaving Josephus behind, while Thornton wove through the shelves. He orated a practised background and description of every item in his collection, boasting of their historical significance or rarity. She would never remember all the details, but she could easily remember the location and name of the most valuable sounding items. As they went through his catalogue she gave murmurs of astonishment and approval, trying to think up

75

intelligent questions.

When they were finished she thanked him with all the sincerity she could fabricate. Back at the table, Tho was placing three plates of food down. She disappeared when it was apparent Thornton had no other requests of her. They sat.

The portions were small and colourful, cowering in a li le arrangement in the centre of the plate, an artistic smear of sauce surrounding them. Penellina kept her eyes from rolling, and spoke as they ate. "There are so many varied and valuable things in your collection. It must have taken a long time, and a lot of money to curate such curiosities. Where do you find them?"

"They tend to find me," Thornton said. "You see, I pay a premium for such items. Adventurers know that if they discover something unusual, they can bring it to me and get a fair price."

"Like the Eye?"

Thornton coughed a li le and looked quickly at Josephus before replying. "No no. Not the Eye. Josephus here is fulfilling a prophecy. The Eye is not for my collection."

"I see," she said. She turned to Josephus. "How long have you served Mr Thornton?"

Josephus looked pained. "I have *served* Master Thornton since I was a small boy. Much of the collection was retrieved by me."

"Yes. All to do with the prophecy of course," Thornton added. "I only keep it here until Josephus needs it."

"So what happens to it all when you... succumb to time?"

"My last will is quite clear. The estate will go to my two children."

Josephus looked down at his food as he toppled a tower of thinly sliced vegetables.

"I see. Where are they?"

"In Orthendine. They are learning from a scholar — Sumevar Saeen — a very gifted man. Very gifted."

Josephus spoke li le for the rest of the meal. Penellina tried to engage him, but all her a empts were met by monosyllabic answers. Thornton seemed completely oblivious to Josephus's mood, regaling her with some of his own adventures. She kept a bright smile on her face.

When the meal was finished, Thornton clapped his hands together. "So, Josephus. You are close to the end now."

"Yes, master. What is the next quest?"

Thornton reached behind himself and pulled a book with a bright-blue spine down from a shelf. He opened it and ran his finger along the page. It was covered in square runes, each like a li le box containing a series of markings. He turned the book a li le toward Josephus.

"See, here. The evil that grows cannot be contained by the Eye alone. You'll need Reirak."

"Reirak?" Josephus asked.

"It's a legendary dwarven hammer. With both it *and* the Eye, the evil in our lands can be dealt with. Then you need to take both magical artefacts to the centre of the Ganther Plains. That's where the nexus is."

Josephus considered the writing. "I'm sorry, master. I cannot read dwarven."

"Oh yes, of course, of course. No ma er, *I* can read it to you."

"Reirak." Josephus looked up and mouthed the name to himself. "Where do I locate it?"

"It's to the east." Thornton traced a line of runes along

the page. "There is a river that runs from the My'ethende Mountains through the Direwood. At the foot of those mountains lies the tomb of the last of the Rockslinger clan. It's buried there." His eyes narrowed as he watched Josephus. "Most dangerous."

"So, we get the hammer and bring it here too? And Josephus needs all these items to contain the evil?" Penellina asked.

"Ah, yes. Yes." Thornton answered.

"He's going to need a cart to get it all out there—"

Thornton snapped the book shut. "You are so very close, Josephus. I envy you. You are the most important person in the world. I only wish there was more I could do for you. Without risking the prophecy of course."

"Don't worry Master Thornton. Fate protects me. I'll return with the hammer and the Eye."

"But shouldn't we take them to the Ganther Plains?" Penellina asked. "You could meet us there with all the other things." She looked back at the shelves.

"No! No, no. Josephus must return here to be given the blessing."

"Oooh." Penellina feigned sudden understanding. "Then of course, I'll make sure we return here first."

THE TEMPLE DISTRICT WAS EVEN more ostentatious than Farald remembered. Human cities were usually built from timber and cobblestone rather than solid blocks of rock — their short lives made them impatient — but up here on the hill, everything was the yellow brown of limestone. It wasn't fashioned in quite the right way, sort of just dropped into place, no care taken to properly shape the joins, but he supposed it was well-done by man's standard.

He and the Vuhsi rounded a corner in the road. It was impossible for a dwarf not to notice the superior workmanship of the Whurgan Ellagg church, but it would be lost on men. The effort was subtle, smoothed corners, bevelled joins — as though the masons were hesitant to make their god's house as glorious as it should be. Were they in a dwarven city, the rock would be carved in an intricate mosaic depicting the dwarven creation, it would stand twenty feet high.

It would demand devotion.

But here the church kept to itself. Never threatening to loom over the neighbouring temples of the gods of men.

Farald held his face like stone as he ascended the two stairs to the door.

"What me?" the Vuhsi asked.

"All strong peoples are welcome here."

All of Whurgan Ellagg's above ground churches kept their doors closed to the sun. The dwarves and their god preferred the darkness of the deep. Farald pressed against the stone. It didn't open. He pounded the brass knocker against the door.

"What do you want?" a voice behind them asked.

It belonged to a dwarf woman, replete with white and gold vestments gathered in the middle by a wide leather belt. Under her arm, she carried a leather-bound tome.

Farald straightened his back and lowered his head. "I seek guidance and knowledge," he said in Dwarvish.

"Don't lie to me," she said.

"I'm not," he said, keeping his voice even. "I seek an audience with Whurgan Ellagg."

"There's a pub just down the road."

A spark of anger broke through in his voice. "This is a

79

church of Whurgan Ellagg, is it not? Canonical law demands you provide the devout with ecclesiastical supplies."

"There's no grog here. Come back tomorrow for mass. You can get a meal then."

"Look," Farald marched down the stairs. "I am a cleric of the twelfth sect. I *require* supplies and—"

"—prove it."

Farald glowered and pulled at the chain around his neck. From within his tunic he pulled his holy symbol, a fist engraved on a golden disk. He flashed it briefly before pu ing it away. "Now let me in."

"I'm sorry," she said, her demeanour changing. "You're the first cleric — aside from me — that's been here since I took over. Every other dwarf has been an outcast."

"Outcast or not. Every dwarf is to be welcomed at a church of Whurgan Ellagg."

"Strong people are to be welcomed. Outcast dwarves have proven their weakness."

Farald held his tongue. "How long have you been here?"

"Forty-seven years." She produced a key and unlocked the door.

Had it been so long since he'd been to Threerun? He was ge ing old. "That's a long time to be away from home. Why are you still here in the human lands?"

She shrugged. "Whurgan Ellagg requests it of me. There's not much to do, though, just odd errands he has me running here in the city." She put her weight against the door. "The gods work in mysterious ways."

Lit only by a low fire in a long, central pit, the nave was what Farald had expected. Detailed carvings of the tales of Whurgan Ellagg covered the walls — the creation of the mountains, the god's carving of the first dwarf he breathed life into, the gift of dark-vision. The firelight moved across the stories, drawing the worshipper's a ention along each passage. A dwarf could spend a lifetime studying these and still not fully understand them, though Farald believed he understood more than most. More than even a king.

"Would you care to speak the midday rite?" The woman closed the doors behind them. She eyed the Vuhsi, but said nothing as she placed the thick book upon a lectern against the wall.

Farald gazed at the runes along the top of the wall. They never failed to pull him in. "No." He hesitated. "You go ahead. What's your name?"

She raised her head in pride, the way all dwarves did when invoking their clan names. "Mori. Mori of Thrabek."

"The Black Pass? It's been a while since I've seen your people. Strong. Devout."

The woman waited for a moment before speaking. "And you? What's your name?"

He sighed. "Farald. Just Farald."

"I see." She looked up at the runes. "But you are still a cleric?"

"I still believe."

"Does Whurgan still imbue you with divine magic?"

"...no. He does not."

"Then what did you come here for?"

"I told you. To speak to him."

She paused. "You want me to cast a divination spell on your behalf?"

"Yes."

"There is a cost involved for non-dwarves—"

"—I told you. I believe."

"But you are not a dwarf. Not anymore."

Farald grumbled, reached into his pocket, and placed a handful of coins into her upturned hand. Neither of them bothered counting it.

"Wait here."

She left the hall via a side door. Her footsteps echoed down the hallway beyond.

Farald sat down on a pew. The Vuhsi sat next to him. He'd forgo en it was there.

"Dwarf god. Strange."

"Is he?"

"Much rules." It looked over to the book the woman had carried in. "Too strict."

"You've got that right. These stories" — he pointed up at the walls around them — "tell of a god that invented rules. Writ them in stone, then walloped them across the head of every dwarf he made."

Farald stared down into the fire pit. "Dwarves believe it's the way we are created. We follow rules. We follow the law. It's what keeps us strong. But it kills us too. It harms so many of our people. So many of them aren't strong enough to carry the burden of being strong. Too many are outcast."

"Still." He looked back up at the Vuhsi. "It's what makes us."

"Be er god have compassion. Help."

"Yeah, you don't get much of that around here."

His eyes fell upon the story of Whurgan Ellagg and how he taught the dwarves to defend their mines from the other denizens of the deep.

"You know, I've fought your people before. In 1284. Before my exile. In the Craven Mountains."

"Long ago. Great great. Great grandfather fought."

"I'm sorry."

"No ma er. Vuhsi forget. Unimportant."

The war with the Vuhsi was one of his clan's most notable ventures. To think it was all but forgo en by his erstwhile enemies... He *was* ge ing old. They sat in silence.

Mori returned, swinging a thurible. Thick tendrils of white smoke swept from it and lazed about in a trail behind her. In measured steps, she walked around the hall, then came to a rest by the fire. She lowered the swaying orb and let the chain find its place on the floor beside it.

She took a seat next to Farald. The Vuhsi remained on the other side of him. In her hand she showed a few gemstones, red and green. He nodded, though he didn't know why she thought she needed his approval. She clenched a fist around them and then spoke an incantation in High Dwarvish.

Not many of Whurgan Ellagg's followers still learned to speak the spells in the old tongue. He murmured in appreciation.

"I'm ready. Ask your questions." Her voice had an ethereal quality to it. Like she was speaking with two voices at the same time.

Farald took a breath. "Have I pleased you these last few years?"

"You have not gained my a ention, no."

The reply stunned Farald. He pulled his wits together and continued. "But I have brought so many people into your grace. Surely you have see—"

"—What you did is not forgo en."

Farald looked at the impeccable cut and shape of the stones at his feet. They interlocked so tightly, not even a sheet of parchment could be put between. Every stone had a place. In time, every stone could be worked to fit. But one caught his eye, it was chipped in the corner, an edge was slightly concave. The mason had lost his way here, but the completed work was made all the more for its flaw. At least in Farald's eyes.

"Should I prevent the Azair Soloth prophecy from coming true?"

"No. Azair Soloth prophecy is paramount. The plans of the gods must not be altered."

What? Something wasn't right.

"But the Azair Soloth prophecy is only a minor prophecy, foretelling the arrival of some evil that is to be contained. Surely it's not important?"

Anger welled in Mori's voice. "The evil is already upon you. The prophecy is to ensure the events to contain it occur."

Fear crept into Farald. "Should I prevent the prophecy of Loexkear Irth—"

"—No."

With a slim thread of hope, he asked a final question, though he feared the answer. "The prophecies are in contention, do you not want me to ensure only one occurs? Should I prevent both prophecies?"

"NO. Do *not* meddle in fate. It is purposeful. It is designed. You are to see to *both* prophecies' fruition."

"But two prophecies spell a calamity. Many will die."

Her voice multiplied. Where it was two it was now a chorus, the voices of his ancestors, all the way back to the first dwarf. "You will obey. See to their completion, and your power will be restored."

Farald stared at his hands. Years ago, those hands could heal the sick, banish disease. With sufficient prayer he could at one time even bring back the dead. A century of travelling the Three Kingdoms — preaching, converting, and spreading

Whurgan's influence hadn't given him back the holy gift.

"That's everything, Mori. Thank you."

The dwarven woman pinched the bridge of her nose. "Ugh. I swear he never takes it easy in there. I think I prefer running his errands." She rose to her feet. "You have the Eye of Aera?"

He nodded. "Yes."

"Then you have everything we need. I'll get together some supplies and my travelling gear."

"That won't be necessary."

"He wants me to help. Dealing with *two* prophecies won't be easy." She smiled. Odd to find a good humoured cleric. Her time away from the mountain homes must have worn the stoicism down. Still, she had her celestial orders.

"I don't intend to finish them."

She stepped back, aghast. "You must. His word is sacrosanct."

"No." He stood and spoke to the Vuhsi. "Let's go find the others."

"You're making a mistake!" Mori called out after them. "Whurgan Ellagg won't allow such blasphemy."

Farald left the door open on his way out.

CHAPTER SIX

Theft

IT WASN'T HARD FOR JOSEPHUS to spot a dwarf and a kobold amongst all the men on the road. The crowd gave the two of them a wide berth. Josephus and Penny were si ing at a table next to the open-air market, enjoying the intermixing smells of a hundred different foods, a small selection of which sat piled on a plate between them. Short gusts of wind flu ered the colourful canvas awnings of the stalls. Voices hawking wares and arguing prices blended with the laughter and screams of rambunctious children. It was great luck to have found a place to sit at lunch time.

"There they are," he said, rising to his feet. He waved his arm until it was met with a nod from Farald.

Everyone sat down so each was on one side of the small, square table. In nearly all of the stories he was told as a child, the hero travelled with a party of stalwart friends. People that would rally to him in his darkest moment, that would raise him up from the depths of doubt and shame. These companions would provide the backdrop of his story, the glue, the comic relief. He smiled at them and motioned to the plate of food.

"You spoke with Thornton?" Farald's voice was terse.

"Yeah, he's a bit of a cunt." Penellina said, reaching for another slice of fruit.

"Penny! Master Thornton is a great man. How dare you say such a thing." Josephus pushed himself up from the table. "Do you have any idea the lengths he's gone to secure the prophecy?" He was sure that was just dramatic enough to bring some tension to events. Every good story needed a steady stream of tension.

"I've got a good idea of the lengths he's gone," she said, glancing up at him. She spoke to Farald. "He says we need to get the Reirak now."

Farald raised an eyebrow. "The what?"

"Reirak, a dwarven hammer of legendary status." Josephus sat back down. "Surely you've heard of it."

"Can't say that I have."

"Well, I'm sure one of your more learned dwarven colleagues would know of it. No maer, we know where it is."

"We do?" Farald asked.

"Yes, it's east of here, near the foot of the mountains. In the tomb of the last of the Rockslinger clan."

"Rockslinger?" Farald knied his brow. "*Azarn*? They are in the west. In the Wentin Range. Very much alive."

"You must be mistaken," Josephus said. "Master Thornton was quite clear."

"He had a dwarven book and everything," Penny added.

"What book?"

Penny looked up at Josephus.

"I don't know," Josephus admied. "I can't read

Dwarvish."

"Thornton bad. Lie."

Josephus looked to his reptilian friend. Many of the heroic stories he'd grown up with told of the sceptical companion who provided opportunity for the hero to be proven right.

"Grilk, please. You are wrong about Master Thornton. I will hear no more of it."

"I agree with Josephus. There's no reason to distrust Master Thornton," Farald said. He looked at Grilk.

"Good. Then we can be on our way." Josephus began to stand.

"Not so fast," Farald said, turning his head toward him. "We should set out at first light. It's a couple days' travel to the east. It would be best to purchase supplies here in town, sleep in a good bed while we can."

"I see no reason to delay—"

"—yeah, I've got things to do," Penny said. "Go a see my old friends. You know?" She looked at Josephus.

Of course. Even his companions had their own stories that needed to be told, as minor as they were. "Very well. We can stay at the Black Dog Tavern. It's quite comfortable," Josephus informed them.

Everyone agreed.

PENELLINA LIFTED THE BLANKET FROM her legs and placed her bare feet on the wooden floor. She'd waited for hours for them all to fall asleep, and had expected her eyes to adjust, but the room was still impossibly dark. She knew it would be too dark when she got up to go thieving, but Josephus had declared that the blinds should be drawn, and Farald had backed him up.

The three of them were snoring loudly in the small room. It clearly wasn't built to hold four beds, but the owner had squeezed them in anyway. Poor use of space really. If it was a halfling establishment, the beds would be bunk beds, leaving a bit of room for dancing.

She eased her backpack out from under the bed and felt around for what she needed. The lantern could go, it was a full moon. Dagger, a must have. Lock-picks, rope, a sack; be er take the slingshot. When she was ready, she put her cloak on and tiptoed across the room to the door.

As she put her hand on it, Farald spoke quietly behind her. "What are you doing?"

She cursed herself silently for not noticing that his snoring stopped. "I'm just going to the toilet," she said.

"Hold on. We need to talk." He got up and walked out with her.

Once the door was closed behind them he looked back and motioned her down the hallway. "I've got a job for you."

"A job?"

"I was going to tell you about it earlier, but Josephus wouldn't give us a moment."

"Oh?" She crossed her arms.

"I need you to break into this Thornton guy's tower. Get that book."

She thought for a moment. "The dwarf book?"

"Yes."

"Why?"

"Because I don't trust this Thornton guy. The Vuhsi doesn't trust him either. Let's see this book that he's ge ing his instructions from."

"So, how much?"

"How much what?"

89

"How much are you going to pay me?"

He looked at her blankly. Dwarves were the worst, they did nothing but dig up gold all day and then pretended they didn't have any.

"We already agreed on five thousand," he said.

"Yeah, to go with you and steal the Eye. But now we're off doing some other weird shit, before we sell the Eye. This is on top of that."

"You're kidding?"

"No. I can get you an itemised invoice if you want."

"Fine. How much does it cost to rob someone?"

"Well, let me think. He's a wizard to begin with."

"A what?"

"He lives in a tower, don't he? That's wizardy. He's got a pre y crafty security system from what I saw today. And he's got some horrible old half-elf hag casting hexes all over the place. All up, with parts and labour, it's going to cost you a thousand gold pieces." She put a finger to her chin and looked up to the side. "Plus incidentals."

Farald's mouth hung open.

"Well?"

"Fine," he said. "Just get in there and bring the book back."

Penellina smiled and held out her hand.

"I don't have it on me," he said. "I'll pay you the money later."

She gave him the stink eye before agreeing. "Fine. But you be er pay up."

Penellina made her way to the stairs. The Black Dog had a separate entrance for the upstairs rooms. She was glad for it, there were too many disagreeable drunken dwarves and other riff-raff hanging around the common room.

"Don't you need your gear?" Farald asked her.

She turned and pulled her cloak aside, showing him her slingshot and dagger. "All set," she said.

"You take all that to go to the toilet?"

She smiled with glee as she bounded down the stairs.

Once outside, she walked with purpose to the temple district, in the centre of the street, so as not to be accused of sneaking. She wasn't surprised to see so few people out and about as it was a weeknight. She knew what to look for — a conspicuous red cloth — but was surprised to not see any guards. Come to think of it, once they were through the walls she hadn't seen any guards. Barlowe may have been a tiny hamlet, but even it had a ratio of one guard to every five residents. Maybe they just had less crime in the cities?

She shrugged her cloak tighter when she reached the stone bridge to the south eeyacht. A blistering breeze flowed over the water and around the ba lements. Once she was under the trees on the cobblestone road of the island, she ducked into a shadow and waited. When she was sure no one had seen her, she began her ascent.

The tree roots provided ample footing and numerous handholds. At the top of the bluff she waited again, peering down to the path beneath and out over the main road. There was no one around.

A faint tickling travelled down her shoulder. She looked down, turning her arm to reveal a fat, brown spider. Penellina stifled a shriek and shook her arm. The arachnid became frantic and ran down to the back of her hand. It held on stubbornly.

Thinking quickly, Penellina smacked her hand against the tree. The spider fell into the leaf li er with a soft sound. Penellina jumped back and peered forward. Something hand-sized scu led toward her. She stepped back and tripped on a tree-root. In a panic, she jumped back to her feet and pulled out her dagger, holding it protectively in front.

A light lit up a window below the cliff, back-lighting a silhoue e. Another came outside, holding a lantern aloft, illuminating its owner's face. An old man, likely sent out by his wife to investigate. He stopped and fiddled with the lantern, closing the hood and producing a single beam of light. Of course these rich bastards would have a mirrored lantern.

She ducked down and rolled flat onto her back as the light got closer. It hovered around the tree, roots, and tower wall — only the angle of the cliff edge kept her hidden.

A familiar sensation teased at her neck. Then travelled up to her chin. She felt the spindly touches of spidery feet quest near her mouth. She shut it tight. The old man frustrated her with his dogged persistence.

The spider crawled over her face. She closed her eyes and felt the heavy abdomen touch her nose as it climbed. It passed to her hair where she lost all sensation of it. When she opened her eyes, the beam was still searching for answers.

After the old man grunted in satisfaction and turned away, she rose to her feet, leant forward, and ruffled her hair. Then she pulled at her collar and flapped her thin leather armour, equally hoping that the spider would fall out and that it wasn't there.

When she was satisfied, she turned her a ention to the tower. A yellow light came from the narrow windows high on the stone wall of the ground floor. That would be the easiest way in. Luckily, the tree whose roots she climbed had a thick branch that ran just outside one.

At the top, she held her hands around her face and

peered inside. One of the chandeliers was lit, but its flickering light revealed no movement within the room. No one sat at the table.

Even though she'd seen no hint of any when she was here before, she checked the window for traps. She ran her fingers along the architrave, tapped it in the corners. Once she was certain there were no mechanisms, she unrolled her toolkit. The inside of the soft leather blanket was lined with pockets and sleeves, each holding an implement of precise larceny.

Taking a long, thin sliver of flexible metal, she passed it through the gap between the window and frame. She gave it a li le wriggle to push through the slight resistance, and then pulled it up with a jerk. The latch popped and the window swung outward. With a careful hand, she felt the wall below the window, it was smooth and would be difficult to climb back up without help. She fetched her rope, tied one end around the branch and tossed the other end into the tower.

After lowering herself down to the floor, she strained her ears for any hint of Thornton or the half-elf, Tho. It was quiet.

When she reached the shelves she laughed softly. She was going to be buying two or even three kingdoms at this rate. She started filling her sack. Thinking back over the long-winded descriptions from before, she began by grabbing what would be worth the most. After a while she realised it didn't ma er what it was, if it sparkled and gli ered, it went in the sack.

She hadn't even cleared the first shelf when the bag was full. Cursing herself for not bringing her backpack as well, she rummaged through the goods. Anything that wasn't adorned with a gemstone was dumped on the nearest shelf. She continued pilfering, but with a now more discerning eye.

With the bag full again, she went to the bookshelf. There it was, the blue book. She took it down and frowned. It was heavy. Too heavy. There was no way she'd be able to make it back up to the window with it and the rest. She looked between it and the sack of riches.

What was one book worth? A thousand gold pieces from Farald. But… it also had the location of other items like the Eye. Considering that artefact alone was worth six thousand gold pieces, and this book must list — she flicked through some pages — a couple hundred artefacts. And their names. Locations.

She hefted it in one hand, then hefted the sack. Her grandfather had always told her to plan for the future. This must have been what he meant. She removed just enough items from the bag until she could fit the unwieldy book. After trying to slug it over her shoulder, she removed the remaining items. She left them sca	ered around on the floor.

The soft padding of feet came down the stone stairs. She darted between the row of shelves and slipped under the table, dragging the sack with the book behind her.

Tho passed the front of the shelves. She wore a flimsy silky shift thing — just fancy pyjamas really — and walked to the middle of the room. Her head turned to look back between the rows of shelves, to the space under the stairs. Penellina held her breath when the half-elf's eyes passed over her.

They paused on her for a moment, but then continued. Penellina sighed.

Then they started looking systematically at the windows at the top of the wall. Penellina's stomach sank. Her rope still hung from the open window.

With an internal groan, she abandoned the sack and

emerged from under the table, padding toward the closest shelves. Tho's gaze still moved along the windows. Penellina's rope was on the other side of the room. She slipped behind Tho and made her way to the window.

With her feet braced against the wall, she rushed up the rope and crawled through the window. She looked down in panic as Tho's head turned. With a slice of her dagger, Penellina cut through the rope, and let it fall back through the window, its silken fibres making no sound. She leapt up and stood balanced on the top of the outside frame.

From within the tower came the sound of Tho walking toward the open window.

"Can't he put anything away?" Tho said.

Penellina peeped down through the window. Only a sliver of Tho's gowned legs were visible. They stepped back. Something was dragged across the floor. A white hand reached out and searched for the window pane. Penellina grimaced and pushed the edge of it with her foot, toward the grasping fingers. They found the latch, and pulled the window closed.

And locked it.

After giving Tho a few seconds to move away from the window, Penellina touched down and peered inside. Her rope remained on the ground, but had been moved closer to the wall. Between the shelves she caught glimpses of Tho moving items around. She looked at each item and then to the shelves, placing everything so each relic was evenly spaced from the others.

Penellina's sack remained under the table.

When Tho finished reorganising everything, she went back upstairs. Penellina frowned. She unrolled her toolkit and set to work on the window again. As she worked the sliver of metal under the latch, her pick snapped. Penellina huffed. These tools weren't cheap. Maybe Farald knew a smithy that could make them for mates rates?

Her second tool snapped as well.

Penellina clenched her fist. She closed her eyes, let her fingers go, and relaxed.

The last tool she had wasn't as thin as the others. She wished she'd used it first, the wood of the window was a li le aged and didn't sit flush. It went up easily until it hit the latch. Working it in a see-saw motion, the latch slowly lifted. At the final moment, the tool snapped.

Penellina threw it to the ground in frustration. Her toolkit didn't hold anything thin enough to get through. In desperation she tried drilling her dagger at the wood, but it would take too long to do it without being heard.

She puffed out a breath and looked up the tower. There were other windows up there on the second floor. The tree was tantalisingly close to those windows as well.

With a shrug, she climbed up the tree just enough to lift her eyes to the bo om of the glass. Unlike the lower floor, this window stood the height of most of the wall. It was dark inside. She pressed a hand against the window and was surprised to find it loose. Biting her bo om lip, she worked the tips of her fingers under the frame, and pulled it open. The latch pointed to the ground, hanging on its one remaining screw.

Penellina slipped her foot inside and found the floor. The rest of her followed it, then waited in the dark. No Tho. No Thornton. She waited for a cloud to shift and allow the moon to light the interior. The room was narrow, both walls lined with bare shelves. A broom stood in the corner next to her.

The only door was unlocked. She winced as the hinges

creaked. She was at the end of a hallway, light from the downstairs candles lit the far end. Staying low, she crept toward the stairs, ignoring the possibilities behind each of the doors she passed.

Except the last door. Low voices came from within.

"Damn it, Tho. It's your only job, I hardly see how it's a problem." It was Thornton, though his voice had no sense of frivolity in it at all.

Penellina couldn't make out the words in the soft murmur of Tho's reply.

"I don't care," Thornton said. His tone told of his exasperation. "If he *is* the Chosen One, then nothing I do is going to stop him. If he *isn't* the Chosen One then we're rich. Rich*er* anyway."

More soft murmurs.

"Josephus has outlived his usefulness. Just get rid of him, please."

Murmurs.

"I hardly think that's going to pose much of a problem. You can get a few things from the alchemists, that will be enough. I'm going to bed. I suggest you do too. You have a lot of work in the morning."

Penellina hurried down the stairs and retrieved her bag. She paused in the faint light and waited for any signs of movement before grabbing her rope, winding it up, and a aching it to her belt. She hurried back to the storeroom upstairs. There were no more voices on the way back.

With a grin, she lowered her book-filled sack down on the rope, and then climbed down the tree. She repeated the exercise to make it down to the road.

This was too easy. Why hadn't she visited a human city before? She might buy Threerun as well as her own kingdom.

Who did you speak with to buy a city? Oh! Maybe she'd buy whatever kingdom Threerun was in.

She whistled on the road back to the Black Dog. She had never been happier in her entire life.

CHAPTER SEVEN

The Black Dog

JOSEPHUS GAVE A BROAD SMILE as he wedged the proffered bread under his arm. He picked up his bag of assorted fruits from the counter, and beckoned the baker a good day. Once he was outside in the street, he looked over his recent purchases — bread, fruit, cured meat — and decided there was enough for everyone.

People always seemed to be out and about in Threerun, and today was no different. He smiled and nodded to faces as he walked, but few smiled back, and even fewer returned the gesture. The denizens of Threerun were a mystery to him; he just couldn't understand why they were so morose.

He backed into the door of the Black Dog Tavern, jugging the goods in his arms as he tried to hit the latch with his side. Everything threatened to fall out of his arms as the door opened unexpectedly. Though it was early, the proprietor was awake and apparently on his way out.

"Ho there, Mr Rafel," Josephus said. "Good morning to you."

Mr Rafel, thin like a coat hanger, with clothes hanging off him to match, grunted annoyance and bumped into Josephus as he squeezed past. Josephus had been staying at the Black Dog between quests for years, and still had yet to become friends with the man. These old timber walls had practically been his home ever since Master Thornton put him out from the tower — an act predicated by prophecy, of course — and despite its sinking foundations and sagging roof, he felt content here.

Josephus started up the stairs, but paused on the landing. Penny was shouting behind the closed door to the room they all shared. Unsure whether he should intervene in the arguments of his companions, he waited outside the room.

Best to give them a chance to sort it out for themselves. Though he had no desire to eavesdrop, the Black Dog's thin walls made it hard to ignore what was being said.

"What do you mean 'cookbook'?!" Penellina did not sound happy.

Farald's voice was calm. "It's a collection of recipes, printed in a book."

"I know what a cookbook *is*. I mean… Fuck! I mean, *what do you mean* it's a cookbook?"

"Mrs Hammersmith's Tastes of Cravenloft Mountains and the Northern Badlands," he said. "My mother had a copy. I think there was a series."

"What's it worth?" Desperation clung to Penny's voice.

"Well… a lot of my friend's mums had a copy too. It was, I think still is, a popular cookbook." Farald paused for a moment. "Okay I'll give you two? Three copper pieces."

Now the argument was over, Josephus decided it was time to surprise them with breakfast. An easy way to ease the tension and help them forget their concerns. A good leader knew how to get the best out of his followers.

Two loud clumps came from the room as he reached for the door handle. He paused again.

"What the fuck are those?" Penny did not sound happy.

"Hm? Oh. Dwarven bibliopegists bind slate or shale under the leather cover. It keeps the books in decent nick, but tends to make them a li le too heavy to carry around."

Penny mumbled something Josephus couldn't make out.

"What was that?" Farald asked.

"I said Mrs Hammersmith can taste my assho— "

"—What now?" Grilk asked.

"Well," Farald said. "This confirms what you told us. Thornton is full of it. The only question is why send us east?"

Josephus pulled his hand back from the door. Why did they question Master Thornton's authenticity? They had no idea who he was, or how much he had sacrificed to ensure Josephus could complete the prophecy.

"You sure there's nothing there? Reirak?" Penellina asked.

"No. Like I said, the Rockslingers aren't a dead clan. They live in the west. There are no mountain homes to the east, the dwarven kings reached an agreement with the elven council hundreds of years ago. The My'ethende Mountains are elven territory, as is the Direwood."

"Thornton bad. It's a trap."

Josephus gasped. Even his oldest, most reliable companion had turned against him.

"Josephus can't really be the Chosen One," Penny said. "He *is* a bit of an idiot. Can we trust anything that Thornton guy says? He's not even a wizard."

"Maybe Josephus isn't the Chosen One. But he has been

completing *both* of the prophecies, and it's ge   ing very near the end. It must be him."

What was this? *Both* prophecies?

"Is him. Muchok, my chief, confirmed."

Thornton had tried to warn him that kobolds were generally considered evil. What despicable plan had they ensnared him in? Just how deep did the conspiracy go?

Penny chimed back in. "Thornton said he was ge   ing rid of Josephus anyway."

How dare she spread lies about Master Thornton?!

"We've only got to keep him fooled for another day or two," Farald said. "I don't know exactly how he's supposed to complete the Azair Soloth prophecy. It will be hard to know when to stop him."

"Chosen One dies for Loex prophecy," Grilk said.

That was the final straw. Josephus leaned back, and with the full force of his righteousness, kicked the door in. It slammed against the wall. Penny jumped in her seat at the table. Farald reached for his war hammer, wide-eyed. Grilk was on a bed, picking at something on its foot.

Josephus threw the breakfast up into the air. "Aha!" he bellowed. "Traitors! Your deceit is discovered!"

"Josephus," Farald began, dodging a wayward apple. "Hold on a moment. You don't understa—"

"Quiet you treacherous priest, lest I remove your poisonous tongue." Where was his sword? There! On the far side of the room with his backpack and shield. He moved toward it.

"Stop acting like an idiot," Penny said.

"Begone from my sight, knave!"

"Wait. Not understand."

Josephus stopped, turned slowly, and glowered at Grilk.

"You," he said, le ing menace lace his voice. "You ungrateful, treasonous turncoat. Were I not such a benevolent master, I would have you put to the sword."

He reached his backpack, and quickly threw it and his shield across his back. The sheathed sword he kept in his hand. When he turned back to the door, Farald was standing in the way.

"Now just calm down a moment and listen."

Josephus noted the Eye si ing on the table in front of Penny, next to Thornton's blue book of prophecies. The audacity of these scoundrels!

"Move aside you two-faced miscreant, before I behead you."

Farald held his arms out to stop him passing. "I can't do that. We need you."

Josephus stepped forward and drew his sword. The scabbard cla ered to the floor. Without giving the dwarf a moment more to act, he lunged forward, being careful to position himself closer to the table. He flashed his blade through the air, startling Penny, then snatched the Eye from the table.

With a smile, he slashed at the dwarf again, pushing him back and opening up the doorway. Josephus moved to the wall and stepped sideways to the door, holding his sword out at the dwarf. His shoulder bumped into the door frame. He stepped to the side and bumped into it again. There was nothing but wall where there should have been an exit.

"No leave. Stay, please. We explain."

"Damn you!" he cursed Grilk.

The only escape now was through the window. It wasn't that far to the ground, and in any case he was the Chosen One of the Azair Soloth Prophecy. Fate protected him from falls just as well as blades. He hoped it protected him from falls be er than it did from traps.

He put his foot to the new wall behind him and launched himself forward, catching Farald off guard. He pushed the dwarf aside and barrelled onward, toward the glass. After two steps, a bright light flashed from outside, bleeding through the window and washing his vision out. He stumbled in the sudden blinding white. When it subsided, daylight and blue sky replaced it. Bits of wood and stone flew through the air as dust and smoke streamed past. He realised he'd been soaring through the air only after his back hit the street.

FARALD THREW PENELLINA — CHAIR AND all — across the room, then heaved the table onto its side. He crouched behind it just as a ball of bright green magic exploded on its other side, shoving the table back into him. In a panic, he looked over its edge for his war hammer, but there were only shards of floor sticking out over the burning rubble of what used to be the w all.

"Heretic! Where is the Eye?" a woman's voice called from the street.

Peeking around the side of the stout table, Farald spied a white robe and shining steel bracers. Mori Thrabek. He put his back against the table and held onto its legs, bracing for a second impact. What kind of magic was she slinging?

"You call me 'heretic'," he yelled out. "Whurgan didn't answer your prayers with a spell like that!"

"Whurgan Ellagg has spoken to you directly. Come down now, with the Eye, and he may spare your life."

Farald glanced at Penellina, cowering in the corner behind a chamber pot. He waved his arm at her until he had her a ention. Her eyes were wide, seeing past him.

"Where's the Eye?" he asked her.

It took a moment for her eyes to focus and her hands to move and pat her pockets. She searched the floor around her, pushing some rubble aside as she did. After a moment she shook her head at him. "I think Josephus has it."

Farald was glad he didn't need to try and bend the truth without lying. "I don't have it," he shouted to Mori.

"Liar!" she shouted back.

"You know I can't lie!"

"Your words hold no more honesty than any other exile!"

"Hey, we're right here. We're helping you know?" The male voice that spoke was slurred, and ended with a hiccup.

Farald risked ge ing onto his knees. He poked his head up. Two other dwarves, both male, stood on either side of Mori. They wore grubby clothes, and their beards and hair were long and shaggy. One of them was the dwarf he'd tried to help by the city gates. He took a swig from a bo le and passed it to the other before speaking.

"Yeah, Norim's right. We didn't have to help you know, but we love ol' Whurgan too much."

"Right, yep," Norim said. "Dwon and I are very devout. Very devout."

"Just do what I paid you to do, you louts," Mori hissed at them.

Norim passed the bo le back to Dwon. He picked something out of his pocket, and held it between finger and thumb in front of him. His free hand wavered around it for a moment while he wavered on his feet. Green flame burst to life between his hands. With the full force of his body, he stepped forward and flung it up at the remains of the room.

It hit the ceiling above Farald, blasting a chunk of the roof away in a shower of debris.

"Can you hit anything? Or are you too damned drunk?" Mori scolded him.

"For fuck's sake, let me try." Dwon passed the bo le back to Norim. He searched a satchel on his side and retrieved a fistful of loose items. The dwarf said something under his breath and threw his hand open toward Farald.

For a split second it looked like his spell failed and he'd managed to do nothing but throw loose pins and bits of glass. But a spark of light lit up and arced between the pieces. A bolt of lightning struck the table, showering Farald with hot cinders. The deafening thunder made his teeth ra le. He jumped up, smothering burns across his clothes and exposed forearms, and frowned at the circles singed into his beard.

He put his hands up in the air. "I surrender!"

Mori smiled like the cat that had cornered a mouse. She put her hand in front of Dwon, easing him back a step. "So you haven't abandoned all sense. Bring the Eye to me."

"Swear to Whurgan, I don't have it."

"By his beard, I am losing my patien—"

"—I. Am. The Chosen One." From the ground between the three dwarves and Farald, a sheet of wood panelling stirred and flipped over. Josephus rose to his feet, sword in one hand, the Eye in the other. His clothes were torn, blood ran down his side. He was facing Farald. "Did you think your magic enough to stop *me*, dwarf?"

"Josephus, I... I'm trying to help you. But I think you be er get out of the way."

Mori took a sharp breath. "The Eye! Give it to me, human."

"What?" Josephus glanced back, eyebrows raised. He

tossed the hair from his face as he turned. "Oh I see. Got your friends involved, too, have you? Vipers, the lot of you. I am the Chosen One of the Azair Soloth prophecy. Get out of my way." He spat blood onto the ground.

Mori's eyes lit up. "You are the Chosen One? You will come with me."

Josephus pointed his sword at her. "No."

The two exiles prepared more magic. Out of options, Farald went to the edge of the room and jumped down, crashing amongst timber beams and broken furniture. As he pulled himself out of the broken wood, he found the shaft of his war hammer pointed toward him. He gripped it with a silent prayer, though to whom he didn't know.

Norim and Dwon's fingertips swirled with magic. They touched their hands, combining and intertwining the spells into something more. It erupted from them in a thick, sinuous tentacle of green and red. Just before it reached Josephus it bent around him, never reaching him, as though he was ensconced in a sphere of glass.

"What's that then, Norim?" Dwon asked, nodding toward their magic's redirection.

"I don't know, Dwon. But more importantly, what's that." Norim pointed up at the sky.

Farald looked up at the half destroyed roof. The Vuhsi stood on the edge of a tile. Its hood was removed, the morning sun's light reflected sharply in its eyes, some magical spell at work. Though Farald couldn't hear its voice, the mouth moved, while its claws weaved a pa ern in the air. An orange ball of compressed fire blossomed to life in front of it. The sphere continued to grow for a few seconds before the kobold hurled it down to the street.

The ball of fire impacted with a blast, knocking the three

dwarves onto their backs. Fire swelled up around them and whirled in the air like a tornado.

Farald grabbed his hammer and charged toward the flames. He brushed past Josephus as a space opened in the inferno wall. It revealed Mori on her knees, covering her face with her arms. Without pausing, he ran straight through the gap and swung at her side. The hammer picked her up and sent her spiralling through the fire.

Keeping the momentum, Farald pivoted on his heels and held onto the end of the shaft with both hands. The hammer crashed into Dwon's rising head, bowling him over, before likewise pu ing Norim back onto the ground.

Satisfied they wouldn't soon be ge ing back up again, Farald moved to return to Josephus. They could still convince him to finish the prophecies, he just needed to understand what was at stake. It was wrong to have kept the truth from him. Farald would need to live with that.

But Josephus was gone.

CHAPTER EIGHT

Escape

JOSEPHUS GALLOPED OUT THE EASTERN gate on a stolen horse, though the handful of coins he tossed into the dirt where he found it helped him to think of it as a heroic, albeit desperate, act. Crowds of people cursed and jumped out of the way as his horse charged toward them. The ramshackle hodgepodge of shanties and lean-tos soon gave way to acres of grassy hills, the serenity broken only by the occasional farm.

Now at a canter, Josephus noticed the trickle of blood down his arm. He rotated his shoulder to see the wound. It had stopped bleeding and would heal on its own. Without a scabbard, he was forced to hold on to the sword. It grew heavy in his hand. He looked for somewhere to house it on the saddle, but didn't want to risk injuring his steed. What kind of hero would he be then?

The dirt road was empty, save for himself, the horse, and the few birds that took flight at his approach. The path wound lazily around the hills, as if unsure where it wanted to go. He didn't expect to see anyone on a back trail like this, but he regularly checked the horizon behind him for any signs of pursuit.

When he was satisfied he was safe, he took the time to gather his thoughts. Everyone had turned against him. The stories sometimes warned of a betrayal, an act that would set the hero back, not only along the path, but in spirit as well. But never did *every* companion turn. And not only had they turned, they had brought in sorcerers too. It seemed as though every possible measure had been brought against him.

Yet, he wasn't going to let it stop him. And how could it? He was the Chosen One. He would overcome all obstacles.

Thinking about everything he had yet to do, he tried to push the horse on, but it snorted and shook its head — this trot would have to be enough for now. The animal could be swapped at the next village — Sunnyvale, if he remembered correctly — for a fresher, more willing steed. He had only to keep ahead of everyone long enough to find Reirak and return it to Master Thorn—

—Master Thornton! Had they harmed him? He wouldn't let his book of prophecy go easily. If Master Thornton was gone, who would perform the blessing? Could Josephus still collect the other artefacts from the tower, or would they be waiting for him there? That snake-in-the-grass, Penny, knew about the blessing.

He travelled for several hours under clear skies, up and down an endless supply of hills. On the slopes down he urged the horse harder, but it would still have nothing of it. It seemed a ski ish thing — probably unhappy with an unfamiliar rider. He leaned forward and gave it a reassuring pat on the neck.

The road ahead curved and cut into a hillside, leaving

steep escarpments to either side, taller than a rider on horseback. The slopes were covered in the broken fragments of rock removed from the road's construction, giving purchase for a few scraggly thorn-like bushes and ample weeds. Rain run-off had worn diagonal ruts into the packed earth of the trail, though they were dry now.

His horse slowed as it rounded the corner. A figure dressed in white stood blocking the narrow way. Josephus worked the stiffness from his sword arm as he closed the distance. It was a woman. She stared down at something in her hands, long dark hair obscured her face. When she looked up at his approach, waves of relief washed over Josephus.

"Tho! I am so very, *very* glad to see you. Tell me, how is Master Thornton?"

Without answering, she tossed a dark orb at Josephus. As it travelled through the air, sunlight glimmered against it, as if it were made of glass. It burst into a silent, blinding light as a wave of force knocked him off the horse. He fell against his backpack with a grunt, the wind knocked out of him. The sword cla ered to the ground nearby as the horse took off down the road.

"No. No, Tho. Not you too. Please, no." She was never warm to him, or even friendly, really. But she was Master Thornton's very own companion. How could she? How much must fate test his worth? She produced another orb from her clothing, though he couldn't tell *how*, and fiddled with it.

Josephus pushed himself backwards across the dirt to widen the gap between them. He pulled his arms free from the pack, rolled it over, and grabbed his shield. The second black orb hit the ground in front of him. He twisted away as it detonated, its silent energy hammered him into the ground. Pebbles and dirt rained around him.

His eyes fell on the sword. He grasped it and struggled to his feet, steadying himself with the hilt, a taste of blood in his mouth.

She advanced, and produced a two-foot long pipe in her hand, pointed toward him. Like the orbs, there was nowhere she could have kept it on her person. It protruded from a black, metallic box she held with the other hand. Something she did made it click.

With a cry of desperation, he rushed her, shield held in front, sword in the air behind, ready for an overhead cleave.

A ring of fire and sparks exploded from the pipe, almost deafening him. Burning stings struck his chest, his neck, his thigh. The shield rang like a bell, ra ling his arm. He was surprised to find himself falling to the ground, his legs having failed him. With great effort, he twisted to land on his side and fell over to his back, arms slumping against the ground. He tried to raise his sword as Tho approached, but his arm was weak.

He coughed up something warm and thick onto his chin. He tried to curse her, to promise her that he would avenge these evil deeds, but words wouldn't come. It felt like something had a hold of his lungs, squeezing his will away.

Sadness covered her face. "I am sorry." She made the pipe click, lowered it to his face, and averted her eyes.

An arm reached around from behind her and slipped a dagger into her side. It came away in a torrent of blood that flowed out over her white dress. She dropped the pipe as she clutched at the wound. Her face was emotionless.

Through the vigne e of darkness closing in on his vision, Josephus watched Penny standing over Tho, looking down at the blood soaked knife in her palm. She let it fall from her hands.

* * *

DESPITE THE YEARS OF CALLUSES built up on his palms, Farald felt blisters forming under the sled's handles. "Keep that bandage pressed tight," he ordered Penellina. "He's lost a lot of blood already."

"It's not working," Penellina said. "It's soaking through. What do I do, Farald?"

Farald glanced over his shoulder at the li er he was dragging. It was quickly fashioned with what was available, a blanket suspended between two branches, all lashed together with rope. On it lay Josephus, the Chosen One, dying. Farald had wrapped a bandage tight against the wound on the man's neck, another around his leg. Penellina straddled him, pressing her weight down over the hole in his chest.

He didn't have long. And they were hours from Threerun at this rate. Farald wasn't sure how they'd caught up so quickly, even with the Vuhsi's shortcuts overland. He suspected the hand of Whurgan had something to do with it.

Farald shouted back at Penellina. "Keep the pressure on, damn you!"

The Vuhsi appeared on the hill ahead, ski ering down the road toward them, its tail low to the ground. "Road safe. No people," it said as it ran alongside. The creature never seemed to tire, they had run all morning to chase Josephus down. Farald was at his limit.

He bellowed at the Vuhsi, "Can't you do anything?"

"I tell you. No heal spell."

"Do you have a coagulation spell? Or a… *damn.* A—a stoneskin spell?"

The Vuhsi shook its head and fell back to run alongside Josephus.

113

"Grilk." Penellina sounded flat, lifeless. "I'm sorry. He won't stop bleeding."

Farald's legs ached as he reached the rise of the hill, his lungs burned with every breath. Before him lay an endless horizon of hills, each as featureless as the last. In the distance he could make out a thin grey line, it might have been Threerun. He dropped the stretcher and checked over Josephus. With a frown, he resumed his position and pulled them off the road, sliding over the grass. South-west, toward the Ganther Plains.

"What are you doing?" Penellina screamed. She leapt up and got in front of him, pointing to Threerun in the west. "We have to get him to a church, to the healers. We have to hurry."

"I know. We have to hurry," he said.

The Vuhsi ran off ahead and scampered up a tree. It stood tall, extended its neck and scanned the horizon.

"We're going to take him to the nexus point aren't we?" Penellina asked.

"It's our only choice," Farald said. "He has to survive until we get there."

"How's he going to do anything even if he makes it?"

Farald looked back at her with all the dwarven stoicism he could bring to bear. "All he needs to do is die. The closer he gets to the end, the less there's a chance something else takes his place."

They stopped after a few minutes. Farald knelt beside Josephus and lifted the bandage. The bleeding had subsided to a slow trickle, but the skin was white, there wasn't much blood left to bleed. Sweat beaded across the Chosen One's brow. He wouldn't live out the day.

"Drip water into his mouth every now and then," Farald

told Penellina.

Progress was slow over the low, weather-worn hills. Smooth, lichen covered rocks broke through the dirt in unexpected places, causing Farald to turn back and find a different route forward. He stopped occasionally, catching his breath while he tended to Josephus. Without Whurgan Ellagg's gift of divine magic, there was li le he could do. He did his best not to jostle Josephus too much.

The Vuhsi took over, but Farad soon grew impatient with the speed the thin kobold could maintain. This was a job for a workhorse. This was a job for a dwarf.

By late afternoon, Farald had pulled the li er out of the hills and onto the limitless expanse of the Ganther Plains. The horizon was flat, covered in an endless sea of waist high, yellow grass. Waves of wind rippled through it, a harbinger of the approaching storm coming from the south. It was a wall of black clouds, lit from within by sporadic flashes of lightning, underneath which a grey curtain of rain hung.

"Soon," the Vuhsi said. "Soon centre."

The grass gave almost no resistance to the dragging sled, adding a new speed to their progress. There was an outcropping of granite in the distance, about twenty feet high. It stabbed into the ground at an angle, like a splinter in the skin of the earth. As they got closer, a cave entrance underneath it came into view. The ground around it sloped toward the opening, as though it was a great drain, fifty feet across.

"Is that the entrance?" Penellina asked, jogging alongside.

Farald nodded.

The Vuhsi ran down the hill and disappeared into the darkness of the cave, emerging sometime later, waving them onward. Once they were at the mouth, Farald dropped the stretcher and collapsed, rolling onto his back. Every part of him screamed in agony. His shoulders felt like they'd been pulled from the sockets and recently set, he flexed his fingers and found he could barely form a fist. He sucked in painful breaths.

Josephus murmured.

"He's awake," Penellina said.

The Vuhsi leaned down and shook Josephus's shoulder. "Save world now. No do prophecy." The Vuhsi looked at Farald. "Die here?"

"Not close enough, I think. Come on, we can lay him down outside the entrance."

As Farald rolled onto his stomach to push himself up, he spo ed a flash of blue light on the edge of the drain. A dark ellipse sprang into existence, its edges spinning, flicking off specks of magical energy. From within it, three figures appeared. It was Mori, flanked by Norim and Dwon. She wore steel plate armour, polished to a mirror sheen, and encrusted by gemstones and inlays of gold and silver brocade. With a mace hanging by a loop on her belt, and the words of Whurgan Ellagg nestled under her arm, she looked every bit the image of a true warrior priest. The other two wore much the same as they had before, but their beards were now neatly gathered and tied off with cord, their hair pulled back and plaited down securely. They stared in awe at the figure between them as the portal closed in on itself behind them.

"It is good that you brought him this far, Farald," Mori said. "Is it too much to hope that you have decided to obey your god?"

"No. I do not obey," he answered, standing in defiance. He felt naked. His chain mail had been lost in the Black Dog, and, not wanting to slow down from the weight, he'd thrown his war hammer away shortly after coming across Josephus. Without the divine gifts he had nothing left with which to protect himself, or anyone else. His eyes flicked over Josephus for a moment.

Dwon peered down at Josephus. "He looks a li   le fuc—worse for wear, don't you think, Norim?"

"I do, Dwon. He's not completing no prophecies looking like that."

The two dwarves once again looked to Mori. She started down, toward the obelisk and cave. They followed close behind.

"Get out of the way, Farald. That man is dying." She cupped her hands together at chest height, a warm glow radiating from between her fingers, as though she held the sun itself. "Allow me to heal him."

"I can't let you do that," Farald said, stepping over Josephus, positioning himself in front of the prone body. "He can't complete any prophecy, too many lives are at stake."

"Fool," she hissed. "Do *you* know what's at stake? Evil must be dealt with—"

"—I know. But these two prophecies are in contention for the Eye," Farald said. "Many people will die."

Mori advance. "Then they'll meet their god."

The Vuhsi emerged from the grass about twenty feet from their side. It threw a glowing ball of ice at Norim, and ran. When the ice hit, it sent a shock wave of icicles and visibly cold air through the surrounding grass.

As Norim fell, Dwon pulled something from his belt and crushed it in his hand. He said something in Low Dwarvish, and a ray of black burst from his left eye. It hit Farald in the shoulder, wheeling him backwards to trip over Josephus and

117

fall flat. Mori appeared in the air above him, her mace held in both hands, high above her head. She landed beside Farald and thumped him in the head.

CHAPTER NINE

The Chosen One

JOSEPHUS AWOKE TO THE SIGHT of an angel. She knelt over him, shining in all the glory of the gods, her hands upon his chest radiated warmth and life. He felt her blessing flow through his veins, filling him with a sense of peace and love, until it pulled the sinew of muscles back together, and rejoin the torn and flayed skin. The agony ripped at his mind, tearing his sanity away. Then it was gone, replaced by a numbness and the memory of the searing pain.

His mind reached back. Enemies were all around, trying to take the Eye from him. He made it out of Threerun, on a horse, then a hill... "What happened?" he asked her, afraid to look upon her countenance.

"There are evildoers trying to stop you from completing the prophecy," she said. She moved her gaze and studied the ground near him.

He rolled his head to the side and propped himself up on his elbows. Farald was spread out in the dirt, looking like a broken doll — a puppet whose strings had been cut. His chest rose and fell, though blood pooled around his head. Cracks of sound and flashes of light filled the air. Josephus looked around, confused.

"You must go now." Mori handed him the Eye of Aera.

Clutching it in his hand, he studied her for a moment, and then looked back to Farald. Though the dwarf tried to prevent him from completing the prophecy, Josephus could no longer muster any anger for him. Flashes of memory sprung to life. A strong hand over Josephus's chest. Bandages. Frantic concern etched in the old dwarf's eyes.

"Help him, please."

She frowned, but nodded.

Josephus rose to his feet and dusted off his elbows. He turned to face his destiny.

Penny stood by the entrance to the cave, arms to her sides, one white-knuckled hand holding a dagger. She winced at a particularly thunderous sound, looking up nervously at the sky behind him. Her mouth moved as though to speak, but she didn't say anything. A second explosion went off in the air nearby. She jumped and tried to run, but only managed a short step before freezing in place again.

A deafening sound boomed overhead. Grilk soared through the air, a beam of blue energy pulsing out from its palm, toward another flying figure. Balls of crimson fire shot up into the sky from somewhere nearby. Dark clouds filled with lightning roiled above them.

Ignoring the ba le raging above, Josephus stepped past Penny and entered the maw of the cave. Darkness took him, plunging him into a silent void. The sounds and lights of magic were gone. He hung there for a moment, unsure what had happened, before an ambient light blossomed around him. He stepped forward but there was nothing but blackness under his feet, making it impossible to judge if he was moving at all.

Before him appeared a pedestal — or maybe it was always there — upon which sat a small hammer and a small statue. The sculpture was of a hand, palm up, fingers slightly curved around an invisible object. The hammer was thin — an artisan's tool — with a sharp point instead of a clawed end. A jeweller's hammer, fine and precise.

With a clarity he didn't understand, he knew what he must do. He lifted the Eye of Aera up toward the awaiting hand.

PENELLINA WATCHED JOSEPHUS ENTER THE cave and dissolve into shimmering air. The whole situation was fucked. A storm had rolled in over them in a ma er of seconds after the ba le started — looking every bit like what she imagined the end of the world would look like. A pair of magical dwarfs started tossing spells everywhere, mostly at Farald — no doubt some more bullshit he'd dragged her into.

She didn't understand everything that was happening, but it was no doubt the prophecy nexus crap Farald was on about. You don't get magical dwarves — and look of course one of them is fucking *flying* now — for any normal adventure. Maybe she should've listened to her grandparents and stayed in the village to learn a trade.

Farald stirred on the ground as the dwarf woman crouched over him. She was doing the same magicky stuff she'd done to Josephus, though she was the one who had laid Farald out like that.

Penellina shrieked and dropped her dagger as another boom exploded above her head. She crouched down and retrieved her blade, scanning the sky for danger. Grilk was flying too, now — cool and normal — in a magic fight. She looked around for somewhere to take cover.

Not wanting to disappear in the cave like Josephus had just done, she instead found a small overhang, low to the ground, near the entrance. She nestled herself under it, quite happy with the long grass that hid her from a passing glance. With each explosion, she got a li le closer to the rock, and made herself a li le smaller under it.

The dwarf woman rose and backed away from Farald. He shook his head, groaned, and pushed himself to his feet. His legs looked a li le unsteady as he straightened his back and took the situation in. His eyes fell on the dwarf woman.

"Do you have *any* idea what you've done?"

"I've done what any true dwarf would do, Farald. I have done what was commanded of me by our god!"

He threw his hands up in the air. "Our god is a megalomaniac! They all are! Thousands of people are going to die if those prophecies come true."

"It is Whurgan Ellagg's will," she said, raising her chin. "Who are we to question it?"

Penellina gasped as one of the other dwarves stepped in front of her hiding place. She breathed a silent sigh of relief, he was facing away from her. Farald had no idea this other dwarf was behind him. Penellina's knife weighed heavy in her hand. First the barbarian-elf, then the half-breed elf…

She shrugged and stepped out. The dwarf was wearing very li le in the way of protection, though his cloak might catch the blade. She opted to stab him in the back of the neck, and raised the blade, high above her head, with both hands in preparation.

As she plunged it forward, something crashed into her and threw her across the grass. She looked up, wide-eyed, but only the dispersing purple remnants of some spell were visible. Grilk and another dwarf shot past her, low to the ground. She stood agape as they climbed toward the violent storm clouds.

She cried out as she was picked up by the back of her shirt. She kicked and struggled until she was tossed a few feet away. Before she hit the ground she twisted so she could land smoothly and roll to her feet. The dwarf she was going to stab stood there, smiling like a sadistic boy who had just caught a frog. He fished around in the satchel by his side.

While he searched for the next piece of whatever spell he was about to incinerate her with, Penellina ran toward him. The dwarf spared her a glance and continued his search with renewed vigour. He found whatever he was looking for and raised it to her, sparks of magic already forming around his hand. At the last moment, she dropped low and dived to the side, tumbling down into the grass. She moved away from her landing spot, on all fours, and circled the dwarf. Fire burst in the place she had been.

When she risked a peek out of the grass, she found he was still scanning the area where she had been. Damn wizards! They weren't any good without their bags of stuff, and spell books. She rushed toward him, sliced the strap of his bag, and took off with it, keeping low once again. He cursed and screamed behind her.

After another abrupt change in direction, she put twenty feet or so between them, stood up, and displayed the bag to him. She couldn't help but smile as though she'd just snatched the last pastry at the dinner table. He bellowed a few curse words she hadn't heard before as she shook the contents out around her. He ran toward her — a male dwarf made mostly of muscle — reminding her she was still only half his size.

With a squeal, she sprinted away from him, head flicking left and right, searching for safety, hoping all the while this one couldn't fly too. Farald was trying to wrestle a morningstar from the dwarf woman. Streaks of magic hurtled from Grilk's outstretched arms toward the flying dwarf. She ran toward Farald.

"Help! There's a magic dwarf after me!"

Farald spared her a glance and then kicked his boot into the dwarf woman's shin. She picked her leg up off the ground. Farald forced her off balance and wrenched the weapon from her grip.

Something yanked Penellina's foot out behind her as she ran. She fell and slid deep into the grass. Turning back to her pursuer, she screamed, he was already atop her. She tried to throw her arms out but found they were caught in the tangle of grass. He slammed his knee down against her chest, arched his back and raised his fists above his head. Penellina squeezed her eyes shut.

A deafening rumble shook the ground under her back, reverberating in her head. She opened her eyes. Everything — the grass, the dwarf, the obelisk — was vibrating in a blur. A terrific ray of golden light sliced through the clouds and lit the top of the great rock above the cave. The light's radiance increased as the incredible sound got louder and louder, making it hard to think. Penellina felt compelled to look at the light, even though it blinded her. The magic dwarf removed his knee, stood, and gazed into the bright beam.

Then it was gone — the sound, the vibration, the light — and standing upon the obelisk, directly above the cave entrance, was a dwarf. He seemed taller than most dwarves she had seen, and wore an incredible suit of armour. It was more splendid than anything she had ever seen in her life, glimmering with silver and gold. In one arm he carried a double headed axe, in the other, a massive rectangular shield, slightly curving in on the sides. Even from this distance, the brilliance of the weapons and armour, the intricate carvings etched across their surfaces broadcasted wealth and importance. Upon his chest he wore the Eye of Aera, embedded into his armour. The reflected light from the dwarven figure dazzled her.

"My lord," the dwarven woman said, dropping to one knee.

Farald turned to face the figure, his eyes were wide, his mouth dropped.

"Holy shit," he said.

ON ANY NORMAL DAY, THE sight of Whurgan Ellagg — embodied on the material plane of existence — would have been unusual. But after his initial shock, Farald reasoned that his former god's insistence that he help complete the prophecies should have tipped him off. The gods can't control fate, but they can send visions and hallucinations to adequately inebriated mortals. With the passage of time ma ering li le to them, they could orchestrate any plans through prophecy and divine commandments.

Whurgan raised his axe into the air and roared. His voice sounded like a choir made of every dwarven war cry that had ever been voiced over a ba lefield. The column of sunlight he stood in expanded, melting the angry clouds above them until there was nothing but an endless, clear blue sky.

When he was done, he regarded everyone. Farald had never felt so small, even when first ordained as a cleric of this god. Even when he had first felt Whurgan speaking through him.

Whurgan spoke in a deep voice, more commanding than even the highest of the dwarven kings. "Rise, Mori Thrabek. The people of the Black Pass are looked upon favourably. They have you to thank."

She couldn't puff up her chest any more than she did.

"But you." Whurgan's eyes fixed on Farald. "You have lost your faith."

Farald stepped backwards.

Whurgan glowered at him. "Tell me. Is your faith still shaken now that I am here?"

"My faith was lost when you insisted on the deaths of thousands." He was surprised by the surety of his own voice.

"You dare question me, mortal?! Do you not know a GOD when you see one?!"

A bolt of lightning struck the ground between them, sca ering dirt and grass into the air.

"Come, Mori Thrabek. We will go to the mountain homes and raise an army. The people of these lands are sinful. Their gods do nothing about the immorality that spreads. We will instruct them in the lessons of the scripture upon our return. We will quell the evil in these lands."

Mori rose to her feet and stepped forward, toward the obelisk on which Whurgan stood. Josephus emerged from the cave, facing her, shock evident on his face. He hadn't yet seen the god on the rock above him.

"I must thank you," he said to her. "Without you I would have surely failed."

His eyes widened again as she floated into the air. He rushed forward, passing under her, then looked toward the god.

"Holy shit," he said.

"That's what I said." Farald stepped to Josephus's side,

126

reached up, and put his hand on the man's shoulder. "Well. You've gone and fucked us all now."

Josephus eyed Farald quizzically before gazing back up at the ascending dwarf.

A horizontal plume of purple flame roared into life from behind the obelisk. It engulfed the two armoured dwarfs. Mori screamed. Farald's eyes narrowed as pain showed on Whurgan's face. *He felt that.*

The Vuhsi rose into the air behind the god, his fire growing in intensity. Farald felt the heat of it scald his face. He held an arm up to shield his eyes.

A glorious roar sounded, and the heat stopped. Farald lowered his arm. Whurgan now faced the Vuhsi kobold. Mori stood by the god's side, she breathed heavily. The god and the Vuhsi moved at the same time, launching spells from their outstretched arms. A line of energy from the kobold pierced through a fast moving, sun-like orb from Whurgan, hi ing the god in his chest. It knocked him back a step, a dark blemish now visible across his armour.

Farald looked around urgently for anything to help the Vuhsi. A sword, a hammer, even a stone. A stone! He picked up a rock and hurled it with all his might. On the material plane a god was mortal. Incredibly powerful; but everything with a corporeal form can be killed. Whurgan could be sent back to where he came from. Farald hoped.

The rock sailed past the god. He didn't even notice it.

"Fuck fuck fuck fuck fuck."

Farald turned to see Penellina spinning her slingshot. She fired and hit Whurgan in the back of the head. He dropped his arms and whirled around, his face contorted in anger and frustration.

"YOU DARE!" His voice sounded like an army.

"Fuck fuck *shitsticks* fuck." Penellina hurried over to stand near Farald and Josephus. "What the *fuck*?" she asked. "What did you *do*?" She looked at Josephus.

A blast of purple fire circled the obelisk as the lizard floated above it. Whurgan moved with great effort, struggling against an unseen force. He broke through the invisible restraint and flung his axe at the Vuhsi. The weapon spun end over end and embedded itself into the reptile's chest with a sickening crack.

The purple magic immediately dissipated as the Vuhsi fell, cloak flapping in the wind. Whurgan, his axe, and Mori disappeared before the kobold hit the ground.

CHAPTER TEN

Death

JOSEPHUS'S BLOOD DRAINED FROM HIS skin as he watched Grilk plummet. The limp body hit the obelisk with a wet whack, then crumpled over the edge and fell into the grass with a thud. Josephus rushed to his companion's side and collapsed to the ground, shaking the broken body.

"Grilk," he said. "Grilk!"

Penny appeared on the other side of the body. "Do something," she pleaded, looking past Josephus.

Farald rushed forward, and touched a bloody limb. He cupped his hands against his chest, and looked up into the clear sky. His arms fell in resignation. "There's nothing I can do. He's dead."

Josephus pulled the ta ered remains of the cloak together, bundling up the broken body as best he could. This was too much. He had completed the prophecy, he had done what fate demanded him. Hadn't he? He felt compelled to place the Eye in the hand, that was what the prophecy called for, didn't it? Why was this the price?

Penny turned away. Farald knelt down at Grilk's feet and pulled at the grass. Josephus was confused at first, until Farald dug into the earth with his fingers. Anger welled up inside Josephus, his grip on Grilk's cloak tightened so much it hurt. This dwarf, this harbinger of doom, had obviously convinced Grilk to betray Josephus. How dare he assume his help was welcome?

Josephus pushed Farald's arms away. He glowered at the dwarf, forcing him back with his gaze, and pulled at the ground himself. If anyone would do this, it should be him. His lack of leadership was what caused Grilk's loyalty to falter.

It took him over an hour to dig the grave, sweat beading along his brow in the hot sun. The storm had soaked the soil, making the dirt heavy. The others remained as they were and watched him. He took his time, ultimately digging more than he needed for such a small body. In truth, he couldn't bear to look upon the remains again.

Josephus let his hands drop and took a steadying breath. He sat up and lifted the bundle.

He lowered the body into the hole, Farald and Penny helped him push the dirt back into place. He wanted to push them both away again, but his anger had been withered down by the digging. They remained silent, save for their heavy breaths. When the deed was done, Josephus sat on his knees and stared at the mound of soil. He spared a glance for Farald and Penny — they were both slumped nearby, watching the hypnotic pa erns of the breeze through the grass.

With the prophecy complete, he felt lost and lifeless. He tried to rile up righteousness within himself, vengeance for the fate of Grilk. Something to drive him on and give him a reason to smite these two betrayers. But it failed him.

In time, the shadow of the obelisk stretched out over the plain, and the se ing sun gave the cooling air an orange hue. All of them had yet to move or speak. Was this what it was to be the hero? To have finally completed the quest? He didn't recall any of the stories having such a bi er ending.

"What do we do now?" Penny's voice was listless.

Farald studied her a moment before answering. "I don't think I can pay you what I promis—"

"—you asshole," she said, without any hint of emotion. "I meant Grilk. Should we say a prayer... or?"

Josephus nodded. "Although Grilk betrayed me" — he glowered at both of them — "before you two poisoned its mind, it was my stalwart defender. I don't think I would have go en this far without its service." He felt a small ember within him breathing back to life.

Farald's voice was dangerously quiet. "Do you understand what has happened here? What you've done?" The dwarf rose to his feet, fists clenched at his sides, his face red.

Josephus met the dwarf's gaze with a set jaw. "I've fulfilled the prophecy of Azair Soloth, as was foreto—"

"—you've brought Whurgan Ellagg into the world on a holy crusade. He's going to smite the evil out of the land, alright. Anyone deemed sinful in his eyes." Farald moved to loom over Josephus, jabbing an accusatory finger at him. "That Vuhsi is *dead* because of you. A hundred thousand more will die. Because of you."

Josephus broke eye contact. Guilt ebbed up from his chest, sticking in his throat. There was no denying the dwarf was a god, nothing else could explain how awesome it appeared. And nothing else could readily explain why Grilk was defeated. "I am th—*was* the Chosen One. I had to. I was

131

the hero. It was ordained. Nothing could have stopped me."

Farald glowered at him and raised a fist, ready to strike.

Josephus made no move to defend himself. He felt the ember die out.

When the blow didn't come, Josephus raised his head. All the anger fell from Farald's face. The dwarf turned away.

"You're right about that. It was folly to think we could have prevented any of this." Farald collapsed back to the ground. "The gods put their plans in motion before time began, stretching over ages of history. We would barely be able to grasp the smallest aspect of their designs. If I had done as I was told, maybe it would be me at Whurgan's side, maybe I—I could grant mercy to people, prevent the coming deaths. If I had helped you, maybe that Vuhs— maybe Grilk wouldn't be dead."

Josephus heard the plea for absolution in Farald's words, but he didn't have the heart to give it. Instead he fell into silence once more and studied the ground. Penny sat watching them both. Her mouth opened as if to speak, but she closed it before any words came.

"You are a priest," Josephus said to Farald. "Will you say something for Grilk?"

"I don't know which god he worshipped," Farald said. "I wouldn't want to get it wrong."

"Grilk has no god," a high pitched voice said. It had a rasp, like the caw of a crow. "Not yet anyway."

Josephus whirled, jumping to his feet. His hand went for his sword but it gripped only air.

Standing nearby was a kobold. It stood tall and proud — at least half a foot taller than Grilk — and wore no clothes save for a loincloth suspended from a strap of thick leather around its waist. On its chest was a series of necklaces,

132

threaded with bone and teeth. The tawny skin of its arms and legs was lined with broad pa erns of red and white paint. It leaned heavily against a long spear, from the head of which hung several colourful feathers that flu ered in the breeze.

"Our god is yet to be born," it finished.

It took a moment for Josephus to recognise him. "Muchok," he said, relaxing. "I am sorry." He glanced down at the grave.

"It wasn't its time. Grilk hadn't fulfilled its role." The kobold turned and stared into the se ing sun.

Farald stepped forward, a hint of anger in his voice. "What do you mean, 'role'?"

Muchok pointed its snout up in the air and drew in a long breath, its eyes glowing in the light of the sun. "Our tribe has many prophecies given to us by each generation's shaman. Seven hatchings ago, one of them told of a tribesman that would learn magic. They were the Chosen One, destined to find our god." Muchok looked back at them. "That was *not* our god."

"At least you hope not," Farald said. "With the plans he has, I'm afraid Whurgan will be soon. Hold on— *Grilk* was the Chosen One?"

The kobold sighed and nodded. "Yes. Grilk was to die at our god's arrival."

Farald spoke carefully. "Well, Grilk is dead, and it found Whurgan. But it told us that Josephus was the Chosen One."

"Yes. I lied to Grilk. Knowing you must die could cause you to hesitate. I thought it best for Grilk to be ignorant. If that was indeed our god, then it is good that Grilk doesn't live to see it."

"Why is the kobold god a dwarf?" Penny asked.

133

"Whurgan doesn't care about race," Farald said. "Anyone can worship him."

"Hold on," Josephus said, raising a hand. "Azair Soloth doesn't speak of any gods."

Muchok made a short barking sound, like a laugh. "There are many prophecies. We speak of a different prophecy."

Josephus felt the ember burst into life. He faced Farald. "If you hadn't interfered…" He flailed his arms through the air in frustration. "Why did you try and stop me?"

"Stop you?" Farald laughed. "We were trying to help you —"

"—At least up until the last moment," Penny corrected.

"Well yeah. We were going to stop you at the end. Didn't want either prophecy to come true."

"Why the hell not?"

"We thought you were the Chosen One in both Azair Soloth and the Loex prophecy. Grilk had the right of it. We needed to stop you from completing either, to prevent something like this happening." He motioned with his hands at the world around them, though it all seemed peaceful enough for now. "In any case, both prophecies said the Eye of Aera was needed to complete them. I don't understand how this happened. How both came true in the same moment."

Muchok interrupted. "You can't prevent prophecy."

"You should've told Grilk that," Penny said. "The whole plan was Grilk's idea."

Josephus couldn't believe that these people — this bi er dwarf and these primitive kobolds — could know more about prophecy than Master Thornton. "If there were two prophecies, Master Thornton would have known about it."

"Master 'cunt' more like it," Penny mu ered.

Josephus ignored her. "This can't be right. Master

Thornton has a *hundred* books of prophecy. He has read them all, several times."

"Yeah," Farald snorted. "We took one. It was a cookbook. The man is a liar."

"What?"

Penny sat back on her hands, with her legs out in front. "Master Thornton's book of prophecy that he showed us? That book?" She gave Josephus a thin smile. "It was a cookbook."

"No," Josephus insisted. "There must be some mistake. You must have stolen the wrong book. Most of the prophecies he has are the original vellum."

"It doesn't ma er," Farald said, a hint of finality in his voice. "It's over. Both prophecies came true."

"Wait, wait," Penny said. "Wasn't Josephus supposed to quell the evil or whatever?"

Josephus stared at them, guilt constricting his chest. Had he? It seemed to him that all he had done was *bring* evil into the world. Was Whurgan evil?

"He has," Farald said. "In a way."

Josephus looked at the dwarf in confusion.

"Josephus used the Eye to bring Whurgan down, and in one action completed both prophecies." He raised his eyebrows at all of them. "You heard the god. He's going to quell the evil, the evil of people who don't worship him directly and abide by his tenants."

"That's why I've come," Muchok said. It turned away from the sun and sat, cross-legged, next to Grilk's unmarked grave. It drove its spear into the ground. "The land told me of this and directed me here. The kobold god, this god, Whurgan, can be killed."

Farald barked a harsh laugh. "No doubt. Grilk hurt him

some with its magi—"

"—I hit him in the head with a rock," Penny chimed in.

"But it wasn't enough," Farald said. "Even Grilk wasn't powerful enough. I don't think anyone is."

Josephus sat by the grave and fixed his eyes on the upturned dirt. All this time, Grilk had the power to hurt a god. He smiled, remembering all the times Grilk saved him. Then he frowned, remembering all the times he'd ordered his friend around. That was no way for a hero to treat his friend.

"There is another prophecy known only to a few of our tribe. It is an extension to the Loex prophecy, one that we kept to ourselves. It speaks of a weapon. A weapon of immense power. With it, the Chosen One of the Azair Soloth prophecy will defeat the god." Its yellow eyes stared at Josephus. "We didn't want outsiders to know that our god could be killed, or how to kill it." It gazed down at the grave again. "We didn't know what our god would be, perhaps that is why we were given the extra prophecy that tells us how to kill it."

This was his true calling. *This* was the ending to his story. He would not only save the world, he would avenge the death of his companion, and redeem himself. He leaned forward. "What must I do?"

"You must travel to the east, to the foot of the mountains. There is a tomb there. Within lies Reirak, a hamme—"

"—you're kidding!" Penny slumped to the ground next to Josephus. She looked at Farald as he too sat down. "I thought you said that was a load of bullshit?"

"I thought it was! Everything else Thornton said about it was lies."

"I told you," Josephus said. "He has many books of prophecy. Just because you mistakenly steal the wrong book doesn't mean he's a liar."

"I didn't *borrow* the wrong book!" Penny snapped.

"What about the half-elf?" Farald asked. "Penellina told me that she worked for Thornton. She almost killed you."

Josephus's hand touched the spot on his chest where the hole had been. "I don't know," he admi ed.

"Maybe we should revisit *master* Thornton," Farald said, rubbing his chin. "He might have more info on Reirak. The original prophecies, as wri en, might tell us more of what's happened. And what will happen."

"Do you think I'm going to let you come with me," Josephus stared at the dwarf, bewildered. "After what you did?"

"Like I said, we were trying to help you."

Muchok drew a pa ern in the soil with a clawed hand. "Grilk knew not what was to happen. Perhaps there has been too many secrets?"

The kobold rose and jerked its spear out from the ground. "Grilk is a spirit now. He does not want for anything anymore. The struggle is over for him. He is at peace," it said. "My people await me. They are eager for news, though they won't like this."

There were yet more chapters to this story. Grilk's death was a turning point. The characters had developed and now needed to work together. Josephus needed to trust these people. "Alright. Let's go then. The sooner we return to Thornton and tell him what's happened, the be er."

CHAPTER ELEVEN

The Thieves Guild

PENELLINA WAS INCREDULOUS. "WHAT DO you mean the gates are closed?"

The guard leered at her, a hand on his hip, another on his chin. "Threerun be closed 'til midday today. They be sweeping out the crims."

"Didn't you do that the other day?" Penellina asked.

His smile was missing a few teeth. "Well'um… there's a lo a criminals," he said, licking his lips. "Not safe for a li'l woman like you. Why don't you wait for a while until I'm off duty? I'll escort ya."

Penellina rolled her eyes and huffed away, weaving between the horses, carts, and wagons that packed the road, back to where Josephus and Farald waited. With one hand, she shooed the excessive number of flies that seemed to prefer her over everyone else, and with the other, shielded her eyes from the sun. The day was already showing itself to be bright and hot.

Farald and Josephus were taking shelter under a small

tree. The wind made leaf shadows dance over them. They sat in silence, facing a li le away from each other, shoulders hanging low. It had been a depressing couple of days walking back here.

"Well, the gates are closed again," she told them. "Sweeping out criminals."

Josephus nodded absently. Farald stared at a wagon on the road.

"They say it'll open up at midday." She squinted up at the sky. "No more than a half hour I reckon."

Josephus nodded absently. Farald stared at a wagon on the road.

"Turns out I'm a princess too. Yeah. They're going to crown me in a big ceremony later today." She waited for some kind of reaction, but they still didn't respond.

She plopped herself down on the dirt in front of them.

"We're going to need to find some more supplies. You two don't even have your weapons, let alone your backpacks." The need to remind them that she was the only one who managed to retain her possessions threatened to burst from her. But she didn't bring it up.

Josephus murmured something agreeable. The wagon still held Farald's gaze.

"I'm sorry," she said. "Grilk was into some weird shit, but it seemed really friendly." She put her hand on Josephus's knee and gave it a squeeze.

Josephus lifted his head and met her eyes. "Grilk was the first adventuring friend I'd ever had. I thought we would save the world together."

"You still might," Penellina said with a hopeful smile. She didn't feel very hopeful though. Something in the back of her mind nagged at her.

"Farald," she said. "Master Thornton was full of it, right?"

Josephus's head snapped up, but he remained silent.

"I believe so," Farald said, tearing his eyes away from the wagon. He glanced at Josephus. "But just how much was truth and how much was fiction? I don't know."

"So… it would be reasonable to say that he manipulated Josephus here," she said. "At least in some small way," she added quickly.

Farald nodded, his eyes narrowing. "Yes, go on."

"Then why are we believing what this Muchok says? How do we know he isn't like… the lizard version of Master Thornton?"

Josephus replied. "Muchok wouldn't lie to me. I saved their village from an invading band of goblins. I'm like a… well I'm a *hero* in their eyes." A bit of colour returned to his voice.

"The Vuhsi don't lie," Farald said. "They are a lot of things, but they aren't liars."

"But Muchok lied to Grilk," Penellina pointed out.

They sat in silence for a moment. Penellina was ge   ing the impression no one had any idea what any of these prophecies were about. For all they knew she was the Chosen One.

Voices and movement on the road told them the gates had been opened. Penellina rose to her feet and brushed dirt from her bum. Sweat trickled down the back of her neck. Flies renewed their incessant a   empts to get into her mouth.

The three of them walked down the road together, wedged between a merchant wagon in front, and a group of elves on horseback behind. Penellina glanced over her shoulders at the elves. They kept their eyes forward and their noses up. She stuck her tongue out at them, and turned away, smiling at the distasteful look they gave her.

"Farald," Penellina said. "There's something else that's been bothering me. What did your god mean when he said he'd raise an army?"

"He's not my god. Not anymore," Farald replied. He kept his eyes ahead as he spoke. "In the mountain homes, things are not as they are here. Life is more structured, more rigid. If *he* tells the dwarven kings to wage war across the Three Kingdoms, they will. Without a moment's hesitation."

"He'll need a sizeable army," Josephus said. "Kalindar alone has a standing army of ten thousand. The Queen could raise another fifteen from the levies if there was a threat. Orthendine and Rivendale together could raise twenty thousand, not to forget the wizards and sorcerers that they'd bring."

"Dwarven armies have dedicated *platoons* of wizards," Farald's voice was dark. "When the dwarven kings march to war, they will bring two hundred thousand troops, plus siege weapons. That's on a normal day. With their god commanding them, there isn't a dwarf who won't march."

"Except you," Penellina said brightly, nudging him with her elbow. "You're my second favourite dwarf."

After passing through the gates, they made their way along the main thoroughfare until they came across the remains of the Black Dog. Crumbled and charred wood lay piled in front of the half of the building still standing. People crawled over it now, picking out what could still be salvaged.

"I suppose we need to find somewhere else to stay," Josephus said.

"Do you know anywhere good?" Penellina asked.

141

Josephus's eyes narrowed. "I was going to ask you the same question."

"Me? How should I know?"

"Can't we stay at your house? Or at one of your friends?"

Shit! It was very rare that Penellina got caught out in a lie. "Yes! I mean… maybe! You wouldn't want to stay at my house."

"I'm sure it's not that bad," Farald said. "I've stayed in some pre y nasty places." He raised his eyebrow at her.

"No. You can't. It's umm…" Penellina looked at the blackened remains of the inn. "Burnt. It burned. To the ground."

"What? When?" Josephus asked.

"Before I left."

"I'm sorry to hear that," Josephus replied. He paused for a moment, looking around. "To be honest, Penny. I've only ever stayed at Thornton's tower or the Black Dog. I don't know of anywhere else. Where do you think we should stay?"

"Yes, Penellina," Farald said, folding his arms. "Can you name an inn we could stay at?"

"Of *course*," she said, adding in a bow with a li le flourish. "We can stay at the Hungry… err… Elf?"

"Which way is it," Josephus asked.

"Follow me!"

Penellina walked in a hurry, desperately hoping they would stumble across an inn. Why was it that you always seemed to be outside an inn, except when you actually wanted one? They were like city guards. She took corners at random until she was thoroughly lost.

"Is it much further, Penny?" Josephus asked.

They were in a quiet street, surrounded by stout

buildings, all built against each other so they shared walls. Each residence was narrow, with two or sometimes three levels. Most of the windows were shu ered despite the weather. With the sun at its zenith above, and the stones of the street below, it felt like an oven.

"Wait here," she said.

She continued on and found a road at a right-angle to the one they were on. A sign hung over the street a few feet away. 'The Hungry Elf Tavern'. She laughed.

"Down this wa—"

A hand clasped across her mouth, silencing her. Someone pulled dark fabric down over her head. She flailed and tried to scream as she was dragged away. She kicked something soft, making it grunt in pain. Something heavy thumped her in the head.

Then a muted voice spoke, "Careful, Grog. Don't want to kill her."

She lost consciousness.

FARALD GLANCED TOWARD THE STREET Penellina had disappeared down and shook his hands out. Penellina had led them into what could only be considered a bad part of town. People here didn't care for their homes, the crumpled buildings and sagging roofs told him as much. Only the desperate and downtrodden were like that. His hand itched for a suitably heavy hammer.

He caught a few glimpses of frightened faces watching through boarded windows, or peering through the narrow gap of a slightly ajar door. What li   le foot traffic there was kept its head down and minded its own business.

Josephus milled about, sniffed, and lifted his boot to check its underside. He pinched his lips and shuddered.

143

Farald should have expected a criminal like Penellina to take them somewhere like this. Criminal types were like homing pigeons, they couldn't help but return to their roosts. Still, he thought he had seen more in her. Maybe he was as wrong about her as he was about prophecy. As wrong as he was about a lot of things.

"Penny," he called out to the street she'd stepped down. "What are we doing here?"

When there was no reply he frowned up at Josephus. "Do you think she's done a runner?"

Josephus's hands pa   ed the outside of his pockets. "It's gone, my purse."

Farald searched his own pockets. "Go— damn it!"

"She's robbed me again!" Josephus strode down to the corner at a brisk pace. "Penny, you kleptomaniac! Where do you get off—"

Farald jogged to catch up. The narrow street was empty. A sign squeaking in the wind read: 'The Hungry Elf Tavern'.

"There," he said. "The Hungry Elf. She must be inside."

Josephus chuckled. "Or she's not, but led us somewhere we could stay the night out of a sense of guilt."

"Right, except we haven't got any money…"

The two of them frowned at each other as they walked up the two stone stairs to enter the tavern. As far as taverns went, this one was empty. And it was not just a lack of patrons — there was hardly any furniture, no fireplace, no candles. A small, fat man sat on a stool at the bar, the other side of which leaned another small, fat man. The former wore the clothes of the working poor — tunic, breeches, and boots — while the la   er wore the tell-tale once-white apron of an innkeeper. Tobacco smoke meandered through the air between them, illuminated by shafts of sunlight from the shu ered windows. The beams came in at an angle, laying odd yellow stripes across their faces.

"Did a halfling woman just come in here?" Farald asked.

The patron lifted his head a li le. It teetered on his shoulder, his eyes were lined in red. "Nah, nothing like that here, mate."

"Damn. What do we do now?" Josephus asked Farald. "The only money I had was in my purse."

The door creaked open behind them. A large being, backlit by the light from outside, side-stepped into the tavern. It stood a good foot taller than Josephus — with shoulders broader than the door. When it stopped in one of the rays of sunlight, Farald felt his stomach drop.

A prominent brow shaded two dark, red eyes. High, pointed cheekbones sat above a sharp jaw line that ended at a wide chin. The upturned nose ended too soon, giving the face an overall skeletal look. Tufts of short, coarse hair burst from the sides of its face. Two incisors poked out from the bo om lip as it spoke, its voice a deep rumble Farald felt as much as heard.

"This is yours," the orc said, tossing two coin purses at their feet.

"You speak Common?" Josephus seemed far more relaxed than he should be. "Oh I see, you're a half-breed."

Farald studied the orc's face again. Sure enough, he didn't have the pointed ears of a full orc, and the arms weren't as long as they would've been were its blood pure. Farald bent down to pick up the purses, never once moving his eyes from the half-orc's face. He too seemed relaxed.

Farald swallowed and kept his voice steady and sure. "Where's Penellina?" he asked.

"Is that her name? She told *me* it was Sarah

Rockfingerer."

Josephus stepped forward and pointed his finger up at the beast. In Farald's estimation, Josephus spoke in a tone far too commanding for when talking to a half-orc. "Where is she?"

"She's being asked a few questions. Was up to no good, without all the proper authorisations and whatnots."

Josephus lowered his finger. "Oh," he said. He winced as he asked, "which guild?"

"Thieves' Guild. But I think you already knew that."

"Can you take us to see her?" Josephus asked hopefully.

The half-orc held his hand out, palm up. "If you want."

Josephus snatched the two purses from Farald and dropped them in the half-orc's hand. "Let's go then," he said.

Farald wasn't sure what had just happened but decided he'd take Josephus's lead. The man had so far shown a great deal of tenacity and luck. All of the trouble he must've gone through in retrieving the Eye... fate was definitely on the man's side, even if Farald didn't understand the whys and wherefores.

"What's your name?" Farald asked the half-orc. It felt very strange indeed to be initiating a conversation with a half-orc.

"Grog."

"I'm Fara—"

"—Don't care."

Josephus's smile beamed. "I am—"

"—Still don't care. Come on."

They followed Grog into the street and down a narrow alleyway. He took what seemed like a series of random turns, sometimes into a wider street, other times through a gate in a fence. Farald thought they'd arrived when Grog took them into a building, only to lead them back out again through a different door.

After ten minutes of this, it seemed they weren't really going anywhere. Just aimlessly walking around.

He leaned into Josephus and whispered. "What's going on?"

Josephus smiled and gestured at Grog. He responded at a normal volume. "He's just making sure we're not being followed, don't worry, we'll be there soon."

"There now," Grog said over his shoulder.

The half-orc rapped his knuckles against a steel door. A li le window slid open. Grog bent his knees to get his eyes at the right height.

"It's only me," he said.

Something clanked and the door swung open with a piercing shriek. Farald hesitated before following Grog inside.

The room looked every bit like the common room of any tavern in The Three Kingdoms — except the one they'd just left. A fireplace in the corner had several pots cooking over it, and tables and chairs were arranged to squeeze as many in the space as possible. Along one wall ran a bar, in front of which several people stood, too involved in their own conversations to pay any mind to the entrance of a half-orc. Farald guessed they were used to this hulking figure coming and going.

At a table in the centre of the room sat Penellina. She was in a chair a li le too far away from the table, downcast eyes staring down at her hands clasped in her lap. Across from her sat a halfling man with grey hair pulled back in a ponytail. He wore clothes that mostly favoured function over fashion, though they looked too well made for a place like this. The point of a dagger sat balancing on the end of his finger as he leaned back.

Grog urged Farald and Josephus toward them.

"Penellina, are you alright?" Farald asked.

"Yeah, I'm okay," she said. All of the normal facetiousness was gone from her voice.

"For now anyway," the other halfling said. He flashed his arm out and the dagger disappeared. "I'm Galan Leafwhisper. Your friend here is in a lot of trouble." He motioned for them to sit at the table.

"What did she steal?" Josephus asked, taking a seat.

Galan cleared his throat. "Aside from your own purses —"

"—that was just for safekeeping," Penellina said. "Tell him, guys."

Galan held his hand up. "Aside from that. She stole something from the tower on the south island."

"Oh that's not a problem," Farald said. "That's Master Thornton's tower. The book wasn't stolen per se, just err—"

"—borrowed," Penellina said, urging him to nod along with her.

"Right, yes. Josephus here" — Farald clapped Josephus on the shoulder — "is Master Thornton's pupil. It's all on the up-and-up."

"It's not that easy," Galan said.

Josephus held out a calming hand. "The problem is she's stolen something without permission."

"As opposed to when you steal something *with* permission?" Farald asked.

"I didn't know about these rules," Penellina said. "Who comes up with this shit?"

"What rules?" Farald asked.

Galan took a deep breath. "No one steals anything in Threerun without the explicit permission of the Thieves' Guild."

Josephus sighed. "What's the punishment?" he asked.

"A hand. If she'd stolen from one of the poorer areas it would only be a finger," Galan said by way of explanation.

"Lucky," Grog said. "Stealing from the temples you lose an arm."

"How much to keep her all in one piece?" Josephus asked.

Galan puffed his cheeks out. "I'm afraid that's not an option. There've been a few too many people doing their own thing recently. The city guards have been forced to crack down on us. Snatched up a few lower-tier crims a few times this week already. We need to be seen se ing an example."

Josephus nodded.

Farald leaned back and surveyed the room. There were more people in here than he originally thought. People sat along the edges of the room, in the dim half-light from the fires. As his eyes passed over them, a few moved deeper into the shadows. What was he thinking? He didn't even have a weapon.

When his eyes fell back on Penellina, she caught his gaze, and gave a brave li le smile.

"I don't want to lose my hand," she said. "I like my hands."

"There must be something we can do?" Farald pleaded. "Surely we can cut a deal?"

"Like I said, we need to set an example."

Penellina took in a shuddering breath. "It's okay you guys. Just go and talk to Thornton about Reirak. Maybe you can convince him to come down here and tell them I didn't steal his cookbook."

149

Galan's eyes widened. "Reirak? Thornton has Reirak?"

"No," Josephus said. "But he knows where it is. We're going to go get it."

"How about you bring it to me, and we let your friend here go?"

"Just like that?" Josephus asked.

Galan leaned forward and tiled his head to them. "Just. Like. That."

"We need it," Farald interjected. "When we're done, we can bring it to you." What kind of games was Josephus playing with these people?

"I'm sorry," said Galan, leaning back in his chair and crossing his arms. "I think there's been a misunderstanding." He smiled. "I'm not negotiating with you. I want Reirak. It will fetch a high price with the right people."

Josephus laughed. "You want us to give it to you so you can sell it to Thornton."

"You're a smart man, you know how things are done around here. Instead of whatever price he promised you, you get Penellina back."

Josephus gave Farald a questioning look.

"Why don't you go get it yourself?" Farald asked. "Grog here seems more than capable."

Grog shifted on his feet and crossed his arms, puffing up his considerable chest.

Galan wobbled his head side to side. "See, the thing is we're not too good in the wilderness and dungeons and everything. Now, put us in a princely manor house and we'd have the silverware in a flash. But good news! We're expanding into hostage negotiation. Give us Reirak, we give you dear Penny."

"I think you need to... sweeten the deal," Farald said,

scratching his beard.

"Farald," Penellina hissed. "It's a good deal."

"He's right," Josephus said. "She's bad tempered, and really quite irritable. Throw in a li   le something extra."

Penellina stomped her feet. "You bastards!"

"You see?" Farald gave Galan an apologetic look.

"What did you have in mind," asked Galan. He leaned forward.

"I could use a sword for starters," Josephus said. "Some new leather armour as well."

Farald nodded. "I need a breastplate and a big fucking hammer if you've got one."

"Anything else?" Galan asked.

Josephus took a deep breath. "Some supplies. A new bedroll. Rope, waterskin, whetstone, flint and steel, a lantern."

Galan gave a flick of his head to someone at the bar. The man nodded and scribbled on a sheet of parchment.

Farald took over. "A pint of oil, a stick of chalk, a few caltrops, a telescopic ten foot pole—"

"—A ten foot pole?" Galan interrupted.

"Yeah, you poke it at the ground in front of you," Farald said.

Galan raised an eyebrow and glanced at Grog. The half-orc shrugged.

"Reirak is in a dungeon. There's usually traps in a dunge — never mind. Lastly we'll need Penellina."

"No, no. You get her when I get Reirak."

Josephus leaned forward and smiled. "You don't understand, she's a part of our team."

"I am?"

"Yes, and we need you to help us get Reirak."

Galan thought for a moment. "Alright. But if you try to double-cross me, then you're dead."

"Does that mean we're in the Thieves' Guild?" Penellina asked.

Galan looked back up at Grog. The half-orc shrugged again.

Galan sighed. "Yeah, I suppose so."

CHAPTER TWELVE

The Real Chosen One

JOSEPHUS PULLED AT THE UNDERSHIRT beneath his new leather armour, shifting it all into place. Penny and Farald walked to either side of him. Their presence and the slap of the scabbard at his side reassured him. The weight of the shield and his full pack gave him hope. He'd always wondered at what drove a man to employment in the Thieves' Guild — surely the jangle of a full purse wasn't enough — but he understood now.

When starting from nothing — both he and Farald had no weapons, armour, or supplies since returning to Threerun — they gave a person a chance. Memories of when he was a street orphan threatened to come into sharp focus. He pushed them back down into the cloudy depths of his past, where they belonged. He was the Chosen One now. And he and his team were fully equipped, ready to tackle the final encounter.

Of course, the moment they'd left the thieves behind, the three of them agreed they wouldn't bring Reirak to Galan and Grog. Josephus felt a li le uneasy with their planned double-cross of the Thieves' Guild, but there was a prophecy to fulfil. They'd bring the hammer to the guild *after* they were finished with it. He was sure the tales told through the generations would either skip this detail or paint it in the right light.

They crossed the stone bridge to the south eyot. To their left was the shaded road that wound up to the tower. Penny leapt in front of him and came to a stop.

"I think we need to talk about Tho," she said, blocking his path. "She killed you."

"I'm not dead, Penny."

"When I was li le, I went for an adventure into the forest. I got lost, with no food, water, or warm clothes. My village sent out a search party and found me in the morning. My grandma was furious with me. I told her I was alright, I didn't understand why she was so upset. She told me to think about what would have happened if it wasn't for the townsfolk saving me."

Josephus was growing impatient, they had a quest to complete, a world to save. "What are you talking about, Penny?"

"If it wasn't for that she-dwarf bitch you would be dead," she said pointedly. "And Tho would have killed you earlier if not for me." She waved her hand up at the tower overlooking them. "And now you're just going to walk right in there and reveal to Thornton that you're not dead!"

Josephus sighed, then took a deep breath. "Penny, I don't expect you to understand. Fate doesn't allow the world to affect me as it does someone of your... importance. Thornton was as betrayed by Tho every bit as much as I was. You will see."

He stepped onto the shadow-mo led path and strode onward. Farald appeared by his side, glints of sunlight broke through the foliage and sparkled off his new armour. The dwarf hefted the new heavy war hammer.

"If it's all the same," Farald said. "I think it best if we be at the ready."

Josephus smiled. Of course his adventuring party was concerned for his safety. He supposed the events that had befallen them served an ultimate purpose in bringing them together. Now that they all understood their place in events, they could finish the story.

He was sure he understood his place now.

"Fine. That's fine. Just, let me do the talking."

Once they were before the steps to the two massive, oak doors, Josephus strode up them and knocked. After a moment of inactivity, he knocked again. When still nothing happened, he smiled at his followers and thumped on the door.

"Master Thornton! It's me! Are you there!?"

"Maybe Tho killed him," Penny said.

The statement caught Josephus off guard. Could that be it? Did her betrayal go that far? She very much intended for Josephus to die.

He resumed his pounding against the sturdy wood. "Master Thornton!"

Farald's boot landed in the centre of the two doors, shaking the hinges. Josephus jumped back in shock. Beyond the doors, something metallic ski ered along the floor.

"He might be hurt," Farald said, shrugging. He took the hammer off his back and raised his eyebrows. "May I?"

Josephus shrugged back.

Penny spoke. "You know we could try one of the windo —"

With a resounding whack from the hammer, something crashed to the ground on the other side of the doors. The left door swung in slightly. Josephus shoved it open and ran inside, Farald and Penny close behind him.

A thunderous boom set off a flurry of sparks and fire on the floor right in front of Josephus. With a panic, he jumped, rolled to the side, and came up with his sword drawn. He'd seen that before, Tho wasn't dead! He scanned the room but couldn't spot her.

A click from within the shelves gave away her position. He rushed along the circular wall. "Farald, take the right flank!"

As Josephus passed the gap between two of the rows, a deafening blast shot toward him. Reflexively, he raised his arms and marvelled at how the li le flecks of light slowed, dimmed, and finally died out as they approached him. Was this some new ability his experience gained him? Some innate magic finally bubbling to the surface?

His eyes focused beyond the flickering flames to the stunned face of Master Thornton pointing a metallic pipe at him, the same kind of pipe Tho had wielded. Beyond his master stood Farald, mouth hanging open, eyes wide. He held his hammer near the ground in one hand, the other reached out to Josephus, sparkles of magic swirling around it .

A rock struck Master Thornton in the head. He stumbled and tried to catch himself on a shelf as he fell into unconsciousness.

Penny walked up and kicked him in the leg. "What a cunt."

FARALD PULLED THE LAST OF the ropes tighter. "There. When he comes to, he won't be ge ing away."

Josephus sat with his hands resting on the table, chewing his bo om lip, on the seat opposite Thornton. Josephus tilted his head in acknowledgement of the knots. Penellina ran her hand along the shelves nearby, taking individual items and stuffing them into a sack.

Farald gazed down at his hands in wonderment. They worked. He'd done something he hadn't done in over two hundred years. Did this mean Whurgan Ellagg had resumed giving him the divine gifts? That didn't make sense! Farald was now trying to kill the god, and besides, he hadn't even prayed for the magic.

He checked neither Josephus or Penellina were paying a ention before flicking his finger at a candle on the table. It didn't budge, ignite, or do anything of merit.

"What are you doing?" Thornton asked groggily. "Think you're a sorcerer or something?"

Farald gave him a clip in the ear as he moved to a seat next to Josephus. "No. But I do have some ques—"

"—why did you send Tho to kill me?" Josephus asked.

"What are you talking about?" Thornton pulled against the ropes. "Why am I bound here?"

"You know damn well why!" Josephus thumped his arm down on the table. "Explain yourself!"

Thornton's face grew red. "I won't be spoken to like that by the likes of you," he blustered. "Explain *your*self. By what right do you invade my home, a ack me" — Penellina cla ered something into her sack — "and *rob* me?"

"I am the Chosen One! I am saving the world!" Josephus looked off to the side. "Again."

Thornton threw his head back and roared laughter. "My dear boy. You *really* are a dolt."

157

"I *knew* it!" Penellina shouted out from the other side of the shelves.

Farald sat back and crossed his arms. He didn't like where this was going.

Josephus's voice was quiet. "What do you mean?"

Thornton laughed. "You're no Chosen One. You're a tool. A muscle-bound meat-head, quick with a sword, and easy to manipulate."

Farald frowned and studied the grain of the wooden table. The prophecies came true; there was a god on a crusade, fighting the evil of loose morals and heathens. Josephus must have been the Chosen One, at least one of them, mustn't he have?

"Do you have the original Azair Soloth prophecy?" Farald asked Thornton.

Thornton's lips pursed.

"He does," Josephus confirmed. "He keeps them all upstairs. They're not pre y enough to display down here."

Penellina's inquisitive voice called out from upstairs. "Are they valuable?"

"Only from a historical context," Farald called back.

She poked her head down the stairs. "But they talk about things like The Eye and Reirak?"

Farald nodded.

"Then they're valuable," she declared. She fixed her eyes on Thornton. "Which room?"

"Third door on the left," Josephus said. "If it's locked, you'll find the key behind an off-colour panel of wood, three steps to the right of it."

"Thanks!" she said with a smile and a chipper voice.

The three men sat at the table in silence. Cracks and bangs reverberated from upstairs, punctuated by an occasional yelp of glee. Penellina rushed downstairs with the sack over her shoulder and an armload of scroll cases. She dumped the scrolls on the table before plopping herself down and rummaging through the contents of the bag. Her eyes rolled up as she took out each item, mouthing silent calculations.

"Which is it?" Farald clicked his fingers in front of Thornton's face.

Thornton's shoulders slumped. "It's marked with green ink," he sighed. "Do be careful, it's quite old."

As Farald looked through the cases, Thornton addressed Josephus.

"Do you remember when I found you?"

Josephus glanced at him before looking away. "No."

"Sure you do, my boy. You were sat in a gu er, asking for alms. I flashed a handful of gold coins at you." Thornton chuckled. "Your li le face lit up in hope. I knew I could use you to manipulate the prophecy. So I took you in. Do you remember that?"

"I remember you bringing me here."

He nodded eagerly. "That's right, that's right. I brought you here and I taught you, did I not?"

"No. You had others teach me. I don't think I ever learned a thing from you."

Thornton shifted his weight back. "Oh now that's not fair, is it? You had the best swordsmen to instruct you. You had the best food. A roof over your head. I did a lot for you."

Farald found the green-marked case. He extracted the scroll with a light touch and unfurled it. His finger ran along the lines of High-Dwarven — why an elven prophecy was wri en in dwarven was beyond him.

Thornton continued. "Do you remember the stories I told

you?"

Josephus remained silent.

"Do you remember the story of Alstair and Aegan?"

Josephus thought for a moment and then met Thornton's eyes. "Alstair was a prophesied hero. Aegan was the wise old man who trained him."

"Yes! And do you remember what happened at the end of the story?"

The prophecy, like most, was wri en so vaguely as to mean almost anything. In particular, the description of the Chosen One was unclear. Many of the words used had multiple meanings.

Josephus spoke. "Alstair fell in the final ba le so that Aegan could destroy the chalice."

"So let me ask you," Thornton said. He leaned forward, his voice became grim. "Who do you think the Chosen One was?"

Farald put the text down and stared at Thornton. A smile broke out across the man's face. Josephus looked to Farald, confusion evident.

"You're not the Chosen One, Josephus," Farald said. "*He* is."

THIS COULDN'T BE TRUE.

"No!" Josephus got up from the table, knocking his chair to the ground. "*I'm* the Chosen One. I... I just completed a prophecy. Assisted in another. I'm working on a third!"

"He's right," Penny chimed in. "That's go a be like a record or something."

Farald read from the scroll in front of him. "And it shall come to pass that the Chosen One, a person of high standing, will ensure events occur which will quell the evil of the world."

"Yes," Josephus insisted. "I *am* of 'high standing', I'm six three. I released the god, I made the events occur."

"No. You didn't ensure anything," Farald said grimly. "You *were* the event. Thornton *ensured* you got there. You wouldn't even have known about it if it wasn't for him."

Josephus tried stepping his mind through everything that had happened. "That doesn't mean *he's* the Chosen One." He pointed at Thornton accusingly. "How in the hell did you read that into it?"

Thornton chuckled. "That's right. I orchestrated events. I made sure you were trained and fully equipped to complete the Azair prophecy."

Josephus's mind raced. There were so many lies. How could he believe anything any of them said? Thornton, Farald, Muchok. Was anything true? "You're the... *a* Chosen One?" he asked Thornton.

"Yes. Prophecies are funny things, you can bend them, shape them. Really quite extraordina—"

"—you can't be the Chosen One! You're nothing like a hero. You've done no good deeds yourself. You don't know any magic, you can't use a sword. You're *fat*! Your hair isn't even blond, it's black!"

Thornton roared with laughter again. He wiped a tear on his shoulder. "They were just stories, you dullard. Fed to you over and over again. All you ever wanted to be was a hero, it was so easy to get you to bring me all these wonderful things." Thornton wiggled his hands bound to the chair, trying to gesture around the room.

"Good thing too," Penny said, placing another item back into the sack. "This should be enough for our entry fees."

Confusion took over Thornton's face. "Entry fees?"

161

"I've joined the Thieves' Guild," Josephus informed him.

"Oh, my boy. You could do so much be er than delve down to their level."

Farald looked up from his reading. "What do you know about Reirak?" he asked Thornton.

"In the case with an orange mark on it," Thornton replied. "It's a scrap of scribbling from someone who heard a story from someone else. It says nothing except where to find it. To be honest, I'm not sure there's anything to find."

Farald read the new scroll, also in Dwarvish.

"I really think you should reconsider becoming a thief," Thornton said to Josephus. "As simple-minded as you are, I always held you in higher esteem than a criminal. You could always take up employment as a guard for one of the nicer inns."

Josephus ignored him. "Is that everything?" he asked Farald.

"It just says what we already know. Reirak is in the east. Follow the river etcetera." Farald tossed the parchment onto the table. "We won't learn anything more here. We should be able to get to Reirak easily enough. This all matches up with what Muchok told us."

"And what I had already told you," Thornton added. "Who's Muchok?"

Farald ignored him. "There's nothing here about any Rockslinger clan though."

"A li le embellishment always gets Josephus in a good mood to go questing," Thornton said with a sly wink.

Josephus was ready to put as much distance between himself and Thornton as he could. "Great. Let's go," he said, rising from the table.

As he made to leave, Farald started untying Thornton.

"What are you doing?" Josephus asked. "Leave him tied. He deserves to starve."

"Didn't you hear what Muchok said?" Farald, keeping his hand on the knots, studied Josephus. "The Azair Soloth Chosen One must wield Reirak to destroy Whurgan. He's coming with us."

Both Josephus and Thornton looked at Farald in shock.

"I'm not coming with you, don't be ridiculous."

"He's not coming with us, don't be ridiculous."

Farald sighed. "Look. You messed around with prophecies, you tried to control them so that you'd get rich."

"He did," Penny said, dropping the last of the items back into the sack with a clang.

"That's right, I did. And the prophecies still came true. They never could have been stopped, so there's no harm in making some money while you're at it."

"That's what I said!" Penny called out.

Farald leaned in close to Thornton. "And now you're going to come with us and help make it right."

Josephus clenched his fist. "N— *Uggggh* — are you *sure*?" he asked Farald.

"As sure as I can be," the dwarf answered. "These two prophecies have been messed around with so much... I don't know."

"I am, most certainly, the Chosen One," Thornton declared. "But I'm not going to help you wave a hammer at a god. Firstly, how do you even expect to hit him? He's in" — he raised an eyebrow and looked at Farald — "heaven?"

"Not anymore," Penny said, weighing the sack in her hand. "Josephus brought him down here."

"You did *what*?" Thornton yelled.

Josephus suddenly found it difficult to meet Thornton's

eyes. "I—I helped complete this other prophecy that brought him into the world."

"Oh my g…" Thornton jumped the chair around to face Penny. "Did *you* put him up to this?"

Penny held her palms out. "Hey, it wasn't my idea. It was Grilk's."

"Grilk? Oh that damned lizard pet. Where is it?"

"Dead," the three of them said in unison.

"Well in any case," Thornton said after a moment. "I'm not going to help you."

"You must," Farald said, loosening the last of the knots on Thornton. "Whurgan Ellagg is not the kind of god you can get along with. He demands devotion and service. The le er of the law must always be followed. Anything other than total obedience is a sin."

Thornton threw his hands up. "What do you expect me to do? I'm not a warrior, I don't know how to use a hammer."

"Can I have this?" Penny was holding the pipe weapon. She waved it at Thornton.

He jumped to get out of the way. "Don't point that at me!" he said. "Put it down! Put it down! You don't know what you're doing, you might set it—"

The pipe erupted in a blast of fire and sparks, blowing a hole through three successive shelves. Splinters flickered through the air as they fell.

Josephus rubbed his ears.

"Whoa-ho-ho!" Penny guffawed. "I'm keeping this."

"Where the hell did you get that?" Farald asked Thornton.

Thornton poked his head up from behind the table. "It's a… I don't know. A whatchamacallit. A—a cannon." He smiled. "It's an alchemical weapon."

"How does it work?" Farald asked.

"Errr... I don't really know."

"This is a pointless waste of time," Josephus said. "We need to keep moving. The sooner we get Reirak the be er."

Farald gave Thornton an encouraging kick as they made their way across the room to the door. Josephus studied his former master. "You know, I'm going to have to train you if you're going to kill a god."

CHAPTER THIRTEEN

Plans

PENELLINA LEANED AGAINST A TIMBER wall as casually as she could in the afternoon sun. She looked down at the sack of riches by her feet with a li le frown, and pushed herself higher up the wall. It was about the agreed time to meet with the guild, a bit early, but she was busy.

Someone walked down the street toward her. She inspected her fingernails and did her best to look like she was uninterested in the pedestrian. This was official Thieves' Guild business. There was a reputation to uphold.

He wore a tunic and trousers, both looking like they'd recently been used to haul potatoes or scrub pigs. His feet were as bare as his head. A sour expression seemed permanently carved into his unshaven face. He stumbled a li le as he walked, probably drunk; definitely a rough kind of person.

"Move along," she said. Her voice held the tone of someone with whom a deal could not be brokered.

His eyes glanced up for a moment as he trundled on.

That's right, keep walking.

She was in the northern warehouse district. Though hardly anyone had any business being in the grid of streets here, the cries of the river men loading their ships at the docks nearby gave the place the illusion of being crowded.

When the coast was clear, she stepped out from the shadow of the warehouse and crossed the street. She rapped twice on an unremarkable wooden door, paused, and knocked out three more taps. It opened an inch.

A voice from within rumbled. "Uhh... the summer breeze takes what it can."

It was Grog. She could smell his breath even through the darkness.

"And it gives nothing back."

The big half-orc stepped back and opened the door up just enough for Penellina to squeeze through. It took a moment for her vision to adjust to the low light. Tall stacks of crates loomed from against the warehouse w alls. Rectangular openings in the ceiling cast three squares of light on the dark floorboards, motes of dust hung in the sunbeams. The space was otherwise empty, except for Galan, standing in the middle of the pools of light, twisting a dagger around his fingers.

"I've umm... got our dues," Penellina announced as she walked over.

"Excellent." There was suddenly no sign of the dagger. "Penellina. I must say I am a li le... curious as to why you've taken up employment with those two."

"Oh it's not as formal as all that," she said. "We just... Well, we were going to sell this golden eye. But it's gone now."

"An artefact, I take it?"

167

"Yeah it was worth at least eight thousand gold pieces." She held her hands out past her shoulders to show how big it was.

"And now you're helping them with Reirak for the money you would've been paid by Master Thornton?"

"Well yeah. Except you said you'd kill us if we didn't bring it back to you instead."

Galan was taken aback. "Not you. No, my deal is with them. You were simply payment."

"Oh!" Penellina thought about it for a second. "Thanks!"

"Why don't you come and work for me after all this is done. I can see you've got some talent."

"Well, I am a master thief."

"Are you now?" Galan turned away and walked in a wide circle around the warehouse. "I take it you were trained in your village?"

"Uh-huh, my grandmother and grandfather trained me."

Galan smiled warmly. "I was trained similarly in my own village. A long way from here, across the seas."

"You're not from the Three Kingdoms?"

"No, I'm from Palaencia."

"No way! I've always wanted to go there."

"You should," Galan nodded. "There's nothing like seeing the homeland for yourself, walking through her forests, farming her soil. It's beautiful." He clapped his hands. "So! Will you come work for me?"

Penellina held a finger to her chin. "I'm not cheap to employ," she teased.

"Of course. Of course." He stopped his pacing. "I tell you what. I'll pay you nine thousand gold pieces if you do one thing for me."

Penellina's eyes lit up. Her heart sang. *Finally some money.*

"It's not quite my going rate... but okay. What do you need?"

"When the three of you secure Reirak, I want you to bring it straight back here. Preferably without those other idiots."

Penellina's mouth frowned on one side. "That's what we were going to do." She didn't mention that it's definitely not what they were going to do.

"Please. I know Thornton is with you now. There's no way he'll part with it once he has it. I've got other buyers interested. Bring it back here to me."

"Nine thousand gold pieces?"

"Nine thousand gold pieces. Now get a move on before your friends wonder what's taking you so long. They're by the eastern gate, waiting."

"Yeah, I know where they are."

FARALD BOUNCED UP AND DOWN on the driver's seat whenever the open wagon hit a pothole or a rut. It was a fine machine, though in his opinion it was a li le under-engineered. He mentioned the lack of suspension to Thornton before they left Threerun. The man didn't care as he'd personally never ridden in it, and never suspected he would.

"Must you aim for every stone on this damned road?" Thornton called out from the back, all sense of affability gone from his voice.

Farald smiled up at the mid afternoon sun and wished for a cloud to pass overhead. Or for a hat to shade him.

"I'm sorry," he said over his shoulder. "Some of the lesser used trails are a li le worse for wear, you know? It's not often the work-crews get onto these."

He pulled the reins so that the heavy workhorse ambled toward a large hole.

Penellina fell into the seat next to him and leaned in close. "This is a silly game you're playing," she murmured. "Not like you at all. What if we break a wheel?"

"I'm sure we can fix it."

"Do you know how to fix a wagon wheel?"

"I haven't got a clue."

Farald caught her off guard with his laugh. He threw his head back and laughed even harder at the look of shock on her face. After a moment more of disbelief, she laughed too and slapped him on the back.

As their laughter petered out, a cloud passed in front of the sun, cooling them. Farald squinted up at it and chuckled. Penellina's eyes followed his.

"You're a changed man... er, dwarf, Farald," she said. "Ever since Whurgan."

"Am I?" he asked. He thought for a moment. "I suppose I am at that. There's a certain sense of relief when you know your god isn't watching you at all times."

"How do you know he's not watching?" Penellina asked.

"I'm fairly certain... hopeful, that he doesn't have omnipotence while in a corporeal form." Farald rubbed the side of his face. "At least that's what I was taught in seminary school."

Penellina nodded. "Silly things, gods. I never worship 'em."

"Don't the halflings have a god? Kinithea Kay... something?"

"Kaylon. Kinithea Kaylon. I don't pay her much mind. She, in turn, leaves me alone."

"I'm afraid things aren't so simple with Whurgan." He shrugged his head to the side. "Well, not anymore."

They travelled over the hills for several hours. Farald

continued steering for potholes. Penellina fli ed about the wagon, sometimes talking to Josephus in the back, sometimes with Farald up the front. Never once did she speak to or acknowledge the existence of Thornton. Farald was thankful for her sporadic company. It provided an escape from his own glum thoughts on what lay ahead of them.

When they reached the cu ing in the hill where they found Josephus, Farald slowed the wagon. He pulled the brake in place and climbed down.

"What are we stopping here for?" Josephus asked.

Flies assaulted Farald as he approached Tho's body. It didn't sit well with him to leave a body like this. Animals had already disturbed the remains. "We should bury her," he said.

"Fuck no," Penellina said. "Why would we do that?"

Thornton stood. "I would appreciate any help burying her," he said.

Josephus hopped down and rummaged through his backpack on the edge of the wagon. He produced a small spade. "Come on then," he said to Thornton.

Farald climbed atop the rocky escarpment and watched the two men dig the grave on the hillside below. Unlike the pliable soil of the central plain, the stony dirt here proved difficult to excavate, but Farald didn't offer to help. It seemed like something these two should do on their own.

When they were finished they asked him if he would speak a few words. She was a stranger to him, and besides, he wasn't really a priest anymore. But still, he obliged and gave a general prayer to the gods, le ing them know she would be with them soon, and to find a place for her in the afterlife.

"Thank you, Farald," Thornton said. "I'm sure she

171

would've liked that."

Farald gave a slight nod. Josephus remained silent with his head down for a moment after Farald and Thornton went back up the hill.

"I found the other cannon!" Penellina said. She stood on the back of the wagon, one cannon in each hand, pointing them up at Farald as he reached the top of the rise. "Boom!" she said. "Gotcha!" She laughed like a maniac.

Everyone climbed back aboard and they set out again, under the pink sky of the late afternoon. Clouds towered over the distant horizon, glowing orange from the se ing sun. There was a flat, grassy area just off the road, covered in wild-flowers, with a few sca ered trees casting long, grey shadows over the field. Farald steered the wagon onto it.

"We'll camp here tonight," he said. "In the morning, we'll pass through Sunnyvale and reach the Direwood by nightfall."

Penellina dropped down and pulled her backpack to the grass. She removed her bedroll and felt around on the ground, tossing stones into a small pile before spreading her bedding out near the wagon. When she was done she did the same with Josephus's and Farald's, positioning them near her own. She checked Thornton wasn't looking, and then kicked the stones out and put his blankets over the top of them.

While Penellina set out the beds, Josephus walked up to a twisted, dead tree and started snapping branches off. He circled the site, collecting more timber in his arms, then piled it between the wagon and the beds.

Farald busied himself with checking their supplies and preparing the ingredients for their evening meal. No doubt Josephus would cook again, he'd cooked every meal on their journey from Grilk's grave back to Threerun. Farald had to admit that the food wasn't bad.

Thornton lowered himself off the back of the wagon and looked for something to do.

Farald held a rope out to him. "Arms please."

Thornton raised his eyebrows. "Pardon?"

"I'm going to tie you up," Farald said. "So you can't leave."

After Thornton was secured, Farald turned his a ention to Josephus. He was striking a flint and steel at a small pile of dried twigs.

"How's that fire going?" Farald asked him.

"Sorry," Josephus said. "Grilk was much be er at this than me."

Farald bent down next to the heap of wood and used his hands to shield the sticks from the breeze. With each of Josephus's a empts to produce sparks, Farald felt his fingers tingle. At first he thought it was the blood returning to his extremities after si ing on the wagon all day, but the prickling became more intense. Just as he was about to investigate his hands, a flash of fire engulfed the twigs. He jerked his fingers back in surprise.

"That's odd," he said.

"What's odd?" Josephus asked, pulling some larger pieces of wood over the crackling flames.

"Did I do that?"

"Do what?"

"That." Farald pointed at the fire.

"Yeah."

"How?"

Josephus sat back on his feet and squeezed his eyes shut. "Let me see if I remember... There are three main magical

173

sources," he recited. "Wizardry, sorcery, and gifts of a divine nature." He opened his eyes and smiled. "I'm guessing, as a priest, yours is the la er."

"Right. Only Whurgan Ellagg wouldn't grace me with any spells. Why would he?"

"Maybe it's another god," Penellina said. "Like, a nice one. Oooh! Maybe it's Kinithea?"

Farald studied his hands and shook his head. "The gods only grant magic to those who worship them. And not just worship. It requires years of devotion and service before a god deigns to notice you, let alone allow you to share in their power."

Josephus frowned at the fire. "Maybe Whurgan is extending a hand out to you?"

"Maybe," Farald said. "But I don't want it."

"Why not?" Thornton asked. He was awkwardly trying to pull a blanket around his shoulders, hampered by the ropes. "With an impossible task such as this, I'd think that you'd want all the help you can get."

Thornton was right, but there was more to it. The only explanation Farald could come up with is that Whurgan was planning something. Giving him the magic only to take it away when he needs it the most. In the final ba le.

"The final ba le," Farald mumbled. He shot to his feet. "Whurgan knows about Reirak!"

Josephus clanged pots and pans as he got ready to start cooking. "Muchok said that the tribe had kept the Reirak prophecy hidden." He sounded entirely unalarmed.

"Then how did *I* know about it?" Thornton asked.

Farald grabbed Thornton by the collar and pulled him in close. "Where *did* you get that scrap of parchment?"

Thornton's eyes were wide. He stammered as he replied.

"A dwarf woman gave it to me. A priest, like you."

"When?"

"Just after Josephus left to get the Eye."

THEY BROKE CAMP BEFORE DAYBREAK, far too early in Penellina's opinion. It's not like Reirak or the prophecies were going anywhere. And it wasn't like Whurgan was at their heels. Farald had promised they'd pick up a hot breakfast in Sunnyvale. She was looking forward to it as the town appeared in the valley below.

From her perch at the back of the wagon, Penellina watched a filthy and dishevelled old man wave his arms in the air and turn around on the spot. He stood in Sunnyvale's town centre — if you could call five buildings a town, and the patch of dirt they circled a town centre. She wondered if any of these buildings were shops that sold fresh food.

As they got closer, his voice got louder.

"The end is nigh!" the old man sang out in a wavering voice. "Repent! Whurgan has demanded it! Repent!" With his arms held above his head, he rushed a group of children who sca ered in fits of laughter and excited screams.

His eyes focused on the wagon. He yelled out again, fixated on Farald, hands grasping out towards the dwarf's feet.

"You, sir! You know what I speak! All those with mountain blood have been told. It's so diluted in me, if I heard him, you must have!"

Farald pulled the horse to a stop. The few people on the road in Sunnyvale had already stopped or slowed on their morning errands. Some looked quizzical, though most watched on with good humour. Farald leaned over and squinted down at the old man.

175

"I know you," Farald said to him.

The old man's eyes went wide with sudden recognition. "Yes! It's you! Farald! Thank you, thank you. Your sermon is what reached me all those years ago!"

"Sermon?" Penellina asked.

Farald flicked the reins and drove the wagon further down the road, out of Sunnyvale. The old man laughed and tried to keep pace with them, mu ering, but was quickly left behind. Penellina looked back at the town as her stomach grumbled. She very much wanted to get a good meal.

"I've spent the last hundred years convincing people to worship Whurgan," Farald said.

"Wow," Penellina said. She started rummaging in her backpack for some dried meat or an apple or anything. "That didn't age well. How many people did you convert?"

"Hundreds? Thousands? After a few years you get very good at it. Humans all want the same thing."

"Yeah. Complete control. Dominance over the lesser folk," Penellina said, shaking her head.

Farald glanced back at her. "What? No. All they want is to know that someone cares about them as much as they care about themselves."

Penellina found a couple of apricots, sat back, bit into one, and thought about what she would do next. With her help, they'd delve into the tomb and find Reirak. Then she'd betray them, run back to Galan with the hammer, get paid. They'd thank her when she split the money with them. What did they think they were going to do? A ack a god? Why couldn't they all just get along?

"Farald?" she asked. "If I converted to Whurganism, would I be safe from his holy war?"

Farald gave her the same look her uncle gave her when

she asked why they don't just mint more money so everyone could have some. "You can't just give lip-service to the gods. They see right through it."

"Right... but if I seriously obeyed his like... commandments or whatever, he'd leave me alone?"

"Yes, he would."

This whole plan — finding the hammer, killing a god, completing a prophecy — seemed more ridiculous the more she thought about it. Nobody had the kind of power needed to defeat Whurgan, with or without Reirak. The image of poor Grilk falling from the sky forced itself to the front of her mind. She wasn't going out like that.

"Farald?" she asked again. "Whurgan is pre y smart, right?"

"Yes, he is a god."

"Right. And so he had the Azair and Loex prophecies set up so that he'd be able to come down from wherever he was?"

Farald pinched the bridge of his nose. "Yes? Maybe. I don't know."

"And he had Mori give Thornton a note to get him to tell Josephus to get Reirak."

"I don't know why Whurgan did that," Farald confessed.

"And he had you going around converting people?"

"No," Farald began. "I was converting people to try and work off my exile." He stared down the road. "But no ma er how many I converted, it didn't seem to ma er. He never again spoke through me or gave me the divine gifts. His few sca ered priests that I ran into would divinate for me, but until Mori, He never replied."

"So, like..." Penellina felt a pang of sadness telling him this. "Maybe he didn't let you back from exile because it was a part of his plan to have more followers ready for his arrival."

Farald opened his mouth to speak but cut himself off. They rode in silence for several minutes.

"I don't know, Penellina," Farald said. "But I think you might be right."

"I don't think we can out plan a god who has had thousands of years to figure everything out," she said.

"I agree, wholeheartedly," Thornton announced. "Especially since I am the one who's supposed to wield Reirak."

"Josephus," Penellina said. "Can you please inform *Master* Thornton that I don't care if he agrees with what I have to say and that he should remain silent until he is asked a direct question?"

Josephus turned to Thornton. "Shut up." He addressed Penellina and Farald. "Prophecies are strange, but they come true. Thornton will defeat Whurgan.... But I have to admit, I don't think him capable."

Penellina jumped at the opening. "So let's just forget the whole thing. Let's get Reirak, give it to Galan, then be on our way." She tossed an apricot stone at Thornton.

"Penny," Josephus said, cocking his head slightly. "You took a long time to pay our dues. Did anything else happen?"

"What? What do you mean?" Penellina splu ered. "There was a puppet show on in the square, and then I ran into one of my old friends." She stood and lifted her chin high. "Despite everything we've been through, you people are all the same! Just because two trained halfling thieves meet in a secluded warehouse does not mean we were up to no good. If you must know we— err— we exchanged Hasput recipes. There was no alternate agreement reached."

"Penny," Josephus said, narrowing his eyes. "What agreement?"

"This is crazy!" Penellina threw up her hands. "You're both insane! You want to fight a god! You want to fight a god who has been planning this since, for all we know, time began. Grilk could fly and shoot purple fire, and Whurgan killed it. *We* don't stand a chance."

Josephus smiled and held his palm out in a calming manner. "Penny, Penny," he soothed. "You're being irrational. You're forge ing that we have a prophecy on our side."

"You weren't even the Chosen One! Fate has never protected you. Just dumb luck!"

Farald nodded in the silence. "We thought it was possible to stop a prophecy, but I don't think you can. I think the few documented times that a prophecy was stopped was probably just misinterpretation. Or more lies to lead us on."

There was no convincing these people. They would convince themselves they were right. An ex-religious zealot who didn't know he wasn't an ex; and a big idiot who couldn't face the fact that he's ordinary. She'd have to take Reirak from them.

Not for the money, but to save them from their own stupidity — though the money certainly helps. She wasn't even sure she'd split it with them anymore.

CHAPTER FOURTEEN

Direwood

Josephus rubbed the balls of his palms against his eyes. "No, no. *Raise* the hammer over your head like you mean to hit something."

Thornton put his weight into it, lifting the hammer high above his head. It wobbled in the air for a moment before his shoulders gave way and it came down. Thornton let go and jumped to the side. The hammer made an indent in the mossy soil.

Josephus threw his hands in the air and turned away. The se ing sun was only just visible over the trees on the edge of the clearing. A wind gently swayed the branches, causing them to dance on the backdrop of the golden horizon. It was cooler here in the woods, the hills they passed over the last few days had been sloping upward, away from the Ganther Plains and into the foothills of these mountains. The trek up the river wouldn't be easy, there was no trail, just increasingly mountainous terrain.

He studied Thornton's soft body. The man wouldn't

make it.

"We already know that Whurgan is probably waiting there. Waiting for you to pick up Reirak. You need to be ready for him."

"We don't *know* that. That dwarf just thinks the prophecy is a trap. Besides, I told you, I'm no warrior," Thornton said, crossing his arms. "Why do you think I had other people train you?"

Josephus sighed. "I suppose it doesn't ma er. If you are the Chosen One, as you say, then fate protects you."

"That's easy for you to say," Thornton declared. "You're not the one who has to rely on some ephemeral sense of purpose for your safety."

Josephus wanted to say he had relied on it for many years. But he wasn't sure that was true now. A sense of pride welled up in his chest; had he completed all those quests through skill alone? By anyone's measure, he truly was an expert adventurer, Chosen One or not. His mind went back over all the people he'd encountered, and what small fragment of skill he'd learn from each. If he stood tall, it was only on the backs of giants. He faltered.

"Why did you send Tho to kill me?"

Thornton turned away and studied the endless depths of trees. Josephus studied the side of Thornton's head, trying to read what li le emotion the man showed. Once, when Josephus was a boy, he thought he'd seen a glimmer of pride when he showed Thornton a new strike he'd learned. But memories like that were few.

"What do you want from me, boy?" he sneered. "Is this where you expect me to divulge some new, secret truth to you? To undo the damage I've caused? To redeem myself?"

Thornton turned back and stepped directly in front of

Josephus. The usual levity in both his gait and his voice was gone, replaced by a cold, hard man. The kind of man who could risk the life of an orphan boy to make himself rich.

"This is no story. I wanted the Eye. I wanted to sell it, or keep it in my collection. That's all. I sent her to kill you, and bring it back."

"Why would sh—"

"—it wasn't the first time she'd killed for me. I was sad to see her dead. She had made me a lot of money over the years. We had become... friends of a sort." The anger in his voice trailed off.

It was simple in the end. Josephus really was just a tool for this man to use. Something he could wield like Josephus could wield a sword.

"Let me ask you something," Thornton said. "Why are you here? You're not the Chosen One."

Josephus struggled to find an answer. There wasn't a heroic story to be told anymore, because he wasn't the hero. But he was no longer an orphan boy si ing in the gu er either. Was he just a minor character? Someone mentioned in passing, a supporting player within a greater person's arc?

"Come on Josephus, it's time to eat," Penny said, emerging from the darkening tree line.

Josephus followed her back into the trees and through the underbrush, not bothering to make sure Thornton followed. For all he cared, the man could run off now. Prophecy was prophecy, it would all happen in the end.

Farald watched them arrive at the camp site and set themselves up around the fire. He waited until everyone was enjoying a bowl of stew before he sat and cleared his throat. "We need to work out a plan for dealing with Whurgan," he said. "Thornton can't fail, he's the Chosen One. Only he can kill Whurgan with Reirak." Farald fixed Thornton with a glower. "And you *will* kill Whurgan." He broke eye contact with the man. "The problem is for the rest of us."

"Why don't we just point him up the hill and be on our way?" Josephus asked.

Farald harrumphed. "Because he'll just run off and do something else."

"Cunt," Penny added.

"He can't 'run off'," Josephus explained. "He's the Chosen One. These prophecies will definitely come true, right?"

Penny looked at Farald, her face lit up. "That's what you said last time! That the Chosen One prophecies are guarantees!" She held her chin up and pouted her lips a li le. "See? I was listening."

Farald watched the fire, leaned forward, and scratched the back of his neck. "Well... you got me there. Maybe there *is* no need for us to do anything."

"Now hold on a minute!" Thornton bumbled his bowl, slopping some of the contents over his fingers. He tried to flick it off his hand. "There's no telling what's going to happen. I *made* myself the Chosen One, I'll have you know. If I was killed on my way up to the mountain, some moron out in the forest may take my place. That's how these prophecies work, it's all bendy and malleable."

Furrowing his brow, Josephus leant over and took Penny's dagger from her side.

"Hey! That's mine!"

Josephus always believed fate protected him. Knowing now it was all a lie, he wondered if fate protected anyone. Could he be the moron out in the forest? He was ready to take Thornton's place. Only one way to find out.

He flipped the dagger in the air, catching the tip of the

blade between thumb and forefinger. With his full body weight, he launched the dagger at Thornton's chest, aiming for the heart.

At just that moment, a bird swooped down, intercepting the blade and bursting into a flurry of feathers. It thumped into Thornton's lap, flapping bits of down and splotches of blood. Thornton jumped up, spilling the rest of his dinner.

"What in the hells!"

Josephus glared at Thornton, a thin smile stretching across his face. "No. *This* prophecy only works for the Chosen One of Azair Soloth. That's you." His eyes fell on the dying bird. "No one else can take your place now."

Penny got up, put her foot on the bird, and jerked her knife free. She grabbed a handful of Thornton's robes and wiped the blade clean. "So I guess we can make like a tree and get out of here."

"Let's leave in the morning," Farald said. "I'm tired. Thornton will complete the Reirak prophecy no ma er what we do. We can sleep in now that there's no rush to get there."

Thornton gathered his senses, frowned, and held his hands out to Farald for the customary rope.

"You can run off if you want," Josephus said. "Fate protects you. If you do decide to run away, it might be easier to run up river. You're going to end up there one way or another."

FARALD STOOD, SURROUNDED BY AN endless expanse of high, tawny grass. In the distance, black, mile high clouds, punctuated by flashes of light, approached him. Wind whipped up from the grass, urging the storm closer. The air was electric with danger. He whirled, searching for shelter, but the horizon remained flat and featureless.

A panicked voice spoke behind him. "Oh god! What do I do?" It was Thornton. His face was stricken with fear as he backed away from the approaching storm. He stumbled and fell.

The storm was upon them now, stinging Farald's face with heavy raindrops. Lightning cracked and struck the ground around them. Again and again.

Thornton screamed and held his hands to protect his face. Then he was gone.

The storm raged on. A thousand voices screamed in pain over the thunder and hammering rain, though they were nowhere to be seen. Their agony grew in volume and overwhelmed Farald, until he too felt the burning righteousness of a god. It seared him with more than just physical pain. Shame and guilt pushed him down to the ground.

A final bolt of lightning struck him. The deep voice of Whurgan laughed.

Farald opened his eyes and sat up calmly. He held his head in his hands; it was slick with sweat. Low tendrils of fog clung to the leaves and ferns around their camp site, driven back by the low embers of the fire. The grey, pre-dawn light found its way through the trees.

Thornton was gone. His bedding and pack missing as well. Farald rose and started rolling his blankets up. He knocked over one of Josephus's pots.

"I thought you said we could sleep in," Penellina groaned. "It's not even morning."

Josephus turned in his bedroll. "There is some flour in my pack. You can make pancakes."

"Thornton's gone. I'm going after him." Farald tied his blankets together and secured them to the underside of his

185

backpack.

Penellina mumbled something as she turned away. Josephus propped himself up on one elbow.

"Why? We went over this. He can't escape the prophecy. I even threw a knif—"

"—I've had a vision."

Penellina sat up and studied him, concern evident. "How much did you take? And why didn't you tell us you had some?"

"No. I— I can't explain it. I just." Farald searched for the words. "I just had a vision. A prophecy. Thornton is going to fail. Whurgan is going to roll right over him, like a storm."

"How do you know it isn't Whurgan messing with you more? Like how he's been messing with your spells?" Penellina asked. "Can we please just forget about all this? Let's go to Southport. We can get on a ship and sail the fuck out of these kingdoms. We can find a new adventure, right, Josephus?"

"We can't," Josephus said. He looked at Penellina kindly. "Prophecies never lie. Thornton will fail."

Penellina stared at the ground, her eyes focusing somewhere beyond. "But the other prophecy said he won't fail."

"I don't know, Penny," Josephus said. "These are the machinations of gods. I don't think we're supposed to understand."

"None of us were ever going to get away from this," Farald said. "A thief, a warrior, a priest... a wizard."

"It's the same in all the stories," Josephus agreed, nodding.

"No," Penellina said quietly. "I'm out. I was going to go as far as Reirak, help you guys out, but... no. I'm going to

Southport and I'm going to get on a boat and get the hell away from here." She bundled her bedding.

Farald watched her pack, saying nothing. After a while, Josephus collected his things too. When everyone was ready, they stood in a circle by the wagon.

"I guess this is where we part ways, Penellina," Farald said with a li le bow. "You have been helpful. If I survive this, I will seek you out. I will pay you what I promised."

"Oh yeah, don't mention it," she said.

"What about you," Farald asked Josephus. "What will you do?"

"Penny. You saved my life when I first found the Eye. It wasn't fate that saved me. It was you," Josephus said, pu ing a hand on her shoulder and squeezing it. "I am sad to see you go." He nodded to Farald. "I'm with this until the end. One way or another, it's my story."

Penellina looked as though she was about to cry. Josephus elbowed Farald and they both climbed aboard the wagon.

"Bye, guys!" Penellina waved as the wagon left.

Farald glanced backwards and watched her turn and walk away. After a moment he spoke to Josephus. "She'll be back."

"Oh definitely. I give her a half day at most."

PENELLINA WATCHED THE FERNS AND saplings part as she made her way across the forest floor. Despite the recent sunny weather, everything was still soft and damp under the interlocking branches. The leaves, sticks, and logs felt squishy. Still, the air was cool. A pleasant breeze fluffed at her hair, and birds sang sweetly in the morning sun.

She'd made the right decision. Continuing on with a

murder-campaign against a god was suicide. Her grandfather had always told her there were two types of liars in the world: those who lie to you, and those who lie to themselves. The former could be counted on, the la er were to be avoided at all costs.

The cost of avoiding these particular ones was high. By not returning with Reirak, Galan, Grog, and the rest of the Thieves' Guild would put an open contract on her. She wouldn't be returning to Threerun any time soon, that much was certain. And she'd be best to avoid any of the other big cities too, where she was sure members of the guild would be on the lookout for her.

She could go home, back to the village... but Penellina didn't quite feel like she was done yet. No. Her new destination was Southport, then a ship to Palaencia. Adventure! If Whurgan did plan on a religious conquest of the *entire* world, well it would take some time. Probably. She'd be able to live out the rest of her life before she ever came across another dwarf. Surely.

Still, she hoped Farald and Josephus would be alright. They were being idiots, but they weren't bad people. And without her they'd have a real hard time of it. Ge ing through a tomb and finding an artefact wasn't exactly in the skill set of someone like Farald, or even Josephus. Especially without Grilk to help him anymore. And aside from Grilk, she was the only one who had hurt Whurgan.

She slowed her pace as she bounded over a successive series of half ro ed logs, unsure what the right move was. Her grandmother had always told her not to make emotional decisions, but to keep her wits about her when things became stressful.

As she mulled on the idea, something caused the hairs on the back of her neck to stand up. She put a hand on the dagger at her side, making sure it was loose in the scabbard, and continued on. The birdsong had ended.

Her head swivelled at the sound of wings flu ering to her left. She caught a glimpse of a bird coming to a rest in a hollow. A twig snapped to her right. Something rustled behind her. She leapt to the top of the next log, whipped out her dagger, and thrust it behind her.

The blade struck nothing. Her eyes darted across the trees and ground. A gust of wind caused some ferns to gyrate.

She breathed a sigh of relief and smiled ruefully at herself. Some master thief she was. Well hold on now, she wasn't being fair to herself. She did sneak into a wizard's tower and steal a book. It might not have been a spell book, and the tower's current occupant may not have been a wizard, but it very well coul—

A tall, slender woman stepped into view. Her skin was pale. Patches of dirt and yellow grime coated the cloth that half covered her. Leaves and sticks were ma ed in her long dark hair, forming a mass that stuck to her as though it was wet. Her ears were long and pointed, and her eyes sat above high cheekbones. Unlike Tho, this elf was full-blooded. A gu ural sound, like a growling dog, rose up from her chest. She lurched.

"Fuck me!" Penellina turned and ran, charging through the forest. She jumped from log to ground with reckless abandon; dived under a fallen bough that crossed her path, vaulted over a second. She grabbed a hold of trees to pivot herself in random directions, not daring to slow down. Every time she shot a glance back, the barbarian elf was close on her tail, faster than the one she'd encountered before.

Penellina skidded to a halt on the top of a rise. Below her

were several more elves. They pointed and screamed at her. Several of them picked up weapons from the ground: swords, knives, thick branches.

Before she could turn and flee once more, the female elf tackled her. As they fell to the forest floor, fingers clawed at Penellina's face, gripping her mouth and pulling it open. A strong hand jerked at her wrist, threatening to dislocate her arm. More hands tugged at her backpack, her boots, her hair. She screamed.

FARALD PULLED THE REINS AND stopped the wagon. The dense forest had finally closed in on the track it had been threatening to close for hours. To their right, the water of the river was white and turbulent, coursing down and around smooth rock in a gully. Ahead of them sat a wall of trees.

"I guess this is it," he said to Josephus.

"What should we do with the horse?"

Farald came down from the wagon, walked to the front, and eased the harness off the animal. "We'll leave it to go about its business. If it's got any sense, it'll head back the way we came."

The two of them checked what supplies and provisions remained in their packs, and continued on foot. At first they seemed to make good speed, but it didn't take long until Farald was struggling over the rocks and larger tree roots. He considered dropping his armour, but he'd been caught without it once before.

They wound their way up the slope, using branches and trunks to pull themselves up. With each step, Farald puffed out a breath and the war hammer strapped to his back knocked out a clang. He stopped to investigate an itch on his forearm and found himself covered in insect bites.

"This is hard going, isn't it?" he said, wiping sweat from his brow. It'd been about an hour since either of them spoke.

Josephus stopped and slumped against a tree, panting. "Yes, it is. Feels good though, don't you think? Ge ing all those kinks out." He gripped his side and winced as he stretched.

"Oh yeah." Farald nodded in agreement though he didn't concur. "I've been itching for a good workout."

"Still," Josephus said, sliding a li le way down the tree. "No need to overexert ourselves. There's a long way to go. We should pace ourselves."

"Couldn't have said it any be er myself," Farald panted.

After a few minutes of catching his breath, Farald pulled his backpack around and found some bread. He broke the loaf in two and tossed the smaller chunk to Josephus, who smiled in appreciation. Farald mumbled about how good the bread was. Josephus gazed out at the forest.

"You know," Farald said, breaking the silence again. "She won't be far behind us now."

"No, no, not far back at all," Josephus said, chewing. He gave a weak smile as he scanned back the way they had come.

Farald nodded and chewed the bread thoughtfully. He took another bite. "Yeah. She was a funny one. Told me you two were a couple."

Josephus's eyes widened as he tore some bread away in his mouth. "Is that so?" he mumbled. "An odd one, Penny."

"Yeah. She was odd."

Silence sat between them again. Farald took smaller bites, hoping to make the bread last longer. "So you weren't a couple?"

"Oh, good grief, no," Josephus said, chuckling. "Could

you imagine?"

"Mm," Farald bobbed his head up and down. He found he was still bobbing it up and down a moment later.

"Guess we should keep going then," Josephus said, rising.

"Yeah. Let's get a move on." Farald grunted as he rose.

The two of them continued up the forested hill, but at a decidedly more measured pace than before. After travelling for a half hour, they reached the peak. Ahead of them the forest lay flat. To their right was the faint roar of the ever present river.

With a sigh of relief, thankful for the flatness, Farald set off ahead of Josephus. Ferns slipped under his jaw as he moved through the trees, tickling and irritating him. He tried to duck beneath them, but the breastplate hampered his movements.

He turned his head sharply as a particularly rough fern tugged on his beard. Movement caught his eye.

"Did you see that?" Josephus asked.

"Mhm," Farald murmured. He slung his war hammer off his back and hefted it as he kept moving.

Josephus moved faster to stay by Farald's left side, sword and shield at the ready. The distinct sound of a stone clacking drew their a ention to the left. But Farald turned to the right instead, readying against any would-be a acker.

Nothing came.

Josephus raised an eyebrow at Farald and gave a half shrug. They continued on.

An arrow thunked into a tree just in front of them. Farald could swear he'd felt the fletching ruffle his beard. They both whirled to the direction it came from.

A tall, slender elf stood before them. He wore green and brown trousers and tunic, with a half shirt of hide strapped across his bow arm. Two arrows were notched. He pointed the bow at a space between Josephus and Farald.

Farald had hoped they wouldn't come across any elves.

"By what right does a noisy dwarf cross the Direwood?" the elf asked.

Farald used the pommel of his war hammer's shaft to nudge Josephus's foot. "I'm only passing through," he said to the elf. Josephus took a step away from Farald.

"That gives you no right," the elf answered back. "Where are you going?"

"To the mountains," said Josephus. "You see I'm the Chose— we're on a quest."

"Wrong answer. You're going back down and out of the forest."

"Look," Farald said, stepping forward — and away from Josephus — I'm an exile. You've nothing to fear from my presen—"

The elf loosed the two arrows. They split away from each other in the air, landing on the outsides of Farald and Josephus. "It's foolish to think you can out flank me," he said to them.

Farald felt the press of a cold point of steel against the back of his neck.

"Especially when you are already surrounded," the elf finished. "Please, throw your weapons down. We will not harm you, we will escort you back to where you entered. Exile or not, we don't wish to start a war."

Farald let his war hammer thud to the ground. He tried to get a look at whoever was behind him, but a pressure on the blade at his neck told him not to. Josephus sheathed his sword and stood in defiance. Farald watched as six elves moved from the surrounding trees and pointed their arrows at Josephus. The elves were there the whole time, right in Farald's line of sight, standing against the trees, completely camouflaged. Farald wondered how many more unseen arrows were focused on them.

Josephus unfastened his shield's strap and let it and the sword fall, apparently changing his mind. "Do be careful with those," he said. "They are only new."

They were marched through the forest at a far greater speed than Farald and Josephus had on their own. It was a winding path, seemingly turning at random, but Farald couldn't dismiss the relative ease of the journey. Try as he might, he couldn't discern where the path was, only that it was there.

Farald held his hand out to brush the plants he passed, disguising his attempt at discerning the nature of the path. A spell to detect magic was simple, he only needed to focus on the area. He expected the warm flow of divinity through his hands, but nothing came. It seemed Whurgan, or whoever, hadn't blessed him with such a spell today. Too many questions, not enough answers.

The elf that had spoken to them remained in front. There didn't appear to be any other elves with them now, but slight flickers of movement at the extremities of his vision told Farald reinforcements weren't far away.

"Do you at least have a name?" Farald asked the elf.

The elf glanced back and after a moment said, "I am Am'yaviasal."

"He who strives the path of good fortune and honey?" Josephus asked with a hint of a laugh. "You elves always have such odd names."

"You know the tongue?"

Josephus said something in what Farald assumed was

Elvish. It sounded lyrical, like a song, but Josephus's tone was not soft. The words went on for some time.

Am'yaviasal stopped on the track and whistled a short bird call. The other elves that had been escorting them emerged from the forest. This time their weapons weren't at the ready. The elf leader spared a look at Farald before addressing Josephus in the common tongue.

"We felt something arrive. But our god speaks to us only through cryptic song. It was definitely Whurgan's arrival?"

"Yes, the Eye was used to bring him down," Josephus confirmed. "I brought him down."

"And you're sure that this hammer, Reirak, will stop Whurgan?" The elf's demeanour changed and he no longer held a tone of threat in his voice.

"Yes. But we need Thornton. He's somewhere in the forest, we think. He'd be headed up river."

"The man you seek, Thornton, was here. We tracked him for a while, but he was taken by the Bael'nindre."

"The what?" Farald asked.

"Charmed ritual guardians... something like that," Josephus explained. "Hard to be exact, Elvish doesn't translate all that well."

Farald shook his head. "What *are* they?"

Am'yaviasal looked away, the hint of a tear in his eye.

"They are corrupted elves. They've lost their way, through no fault of their own. They are not themselves. They came into the forest some days ago. We're not sure what they're doing here."

Josephus rubbed the back of his head and studied the ground, fiddling the toe of his boot at the soil. "So... are they, like, evil?"

Am'yaviasal's eyes widened in shock. "No! Unnatural

magic has compelled them to forget their song. Though they a ack us on sight, we stay back and keep tabs on them. One day the magic that holds them may be released."

"Riiiight," Josephus said, eyes staring past everyone. "Where do they come from?"

"They take anyone of elven kind, and corrupt them. We don't know how. But any elf caught by them, we soon see travelling with them."

"Thornton isn't an elf. Why did they capture him?" Farald asked.

Am'yaviasal lowered his eyes and spoke softly. "To be eaten."

Josephus took a deep breath. "We need to rescue him. He's the only one who can wield Reirak and destroy Whurgan. We think." He gave the elf a pained smile. "Will you help?"

"Yes. If the Eye of Aera has been used to awaken this god, elves must now act."

Farald rolled his eyes. "Don't tell me. You have a prophecy about it."

"What? No. No, we don't believe in prophecies," he chuckled, along with a few of the elves mulling around. "They're just the scribbled ramblings of drunk bards. Half finished songs at best. It's not our fault everyone takes them so seriously."

"Then why are you so eager to help?" Farald's upbringing was hard to shake; you can't trust an elf.

"Because we made the Eye of Aera. It's the right thing to do."

CHAPTER FIFTEEN

Barbarians

PENELLINA COWERED IN THE CORNER of the makeshift cage. The elf barbarians had constructed it quickly, tearing supple branches off of nearby trees, stripping bark from saplings, and lashing it all together. She was tossed inside while it was still being built, all the while they barked and grunted at each other.

They lit a fire nearby, and with the same urgent ferocity, crafted what looked like a spit to roast something, or someone. She scanned the surroundings, hopeful for any signs of game. There was none.

"Shitsticks."

She grabbed the sides of the cage and shook it. There was a lot of give in it, but what did it ma er, she was surrounded by elves. Her eyes fell on her backpack a few feet away. The elves had been largely disinterested in it, dumping it on the ground without checking through it. Two pipes stuck out through the half-opened flap.

By holding the sides of the cage, and standing her feet

197

over the bars on the ground, she was able to jump, and make the cage hop. She did this once. Twice. None of the elves paid her any a ention, more interested in jabbering at each other and shoving. She gave a more daring hop and crossed half the remaining distance.

An elf stepped between her and the backpack. She turned her head up to it sheepishly. It snarled at her and kicked the cage.

"Oh! Look over there," Penellina said, pointing at the other elves.

The elf's head shot to the direction she pointed, and its eyes narrowed. It stalked forward, toward three arguing elves. It gave one a shove and started its own argument.

Penellina made another jump, then another. With her arm outstretched, her fingertips brushed against the edge of the backpack's fabric. She pushed her arm through the bars further, using her free arm to bend the opening wider. Her finger hooked the fabric. She winced as she strained, inching it closer.

A sudden pain shot up her arm. The elf from before stood on it, seemingly oblivious to what was under its bare feet. She cried out and tried to jerk her arm free.

The sudden movement brought the elf's a ention to Penellina. It was female, with oily white hair that hung down in lanky clumps around her face. A glimmer of recognition passed over her eyes as she studied Penellina. She followed the path of Penellina's reach and noticed the bag. With a long hissing sound she knelt down and emptied the bag onto the forest floor.

Every item was picked up, given a cursory glance, and then flung away. The lantern Penellina's grandmother had so lovingly crafted broke against a nearby stone. Penellina's heart sank.

The elf pulled out one of the cannons. She stood and moved the item about, an odd look of curiosity on her face. When the nature of the thing didn't immediately become apparent, she got angry and started to hit the pipe and the box at the end.

Penellina winced.

The cannon erupted, blasting holes in two nearby elves. Everything became silent as all eyes focused on the cannon.

A male elf grabbed the cannon from the female elf and gave her a shove. The female elf shoved back. Another elf came forward and grabbed a hold of the cannon. It was shoved. More elves joined. Soon, almost every elf was fighting. The melee moved further away.

Penellina jumped her cage closer to her backpack, then used her weight to jerk the cage up, and roll it forward. She landed on her head, but the cage leaned against the pile of her possessions now.

She rummaged through it until she found an old dagger. Thankful the fight was still continuing, she made quick work of the cage's bindings.

Keeping low to the ground, she grabbed her backpack, and stuffed whatever was within arms reach back inside. She checked the other cannon for damage, then tucked it under her arm. A few items, including the rope and her lock picks, couldn't be found. She cursed under her breath. What kind of master thief lost their rope and picks?

A few elves grunted and moved away from the fight, back to whatever they were doing before the brawl had started. One turned and walked directly toward her. The elf took a moment to register that she was out of the cage. It pointed and roared at her, signalling all elves to follow its

199

finger.

Every elf ran straight at her. She hefted the remaining cannon, pointed it at the centre of the crowd, and pulled the trigger.

"Fuckin' elves."

JOSEPHUS STOPPED IN HIS TRACKS at the report of the cannon. Am'yaviasal came up alongside him. Josephus could've sworn the low plants of the forest floor moved themselves from under the elf's light footsteps. He moved like a wraith, never seeming to fully touch the ground, every movement smooth and flowing. Very unlike the corrupted elves he'd encountered with the Eye.

"What was that?" Am'yaviasal asked, his voice almost a whisper.

A second explosion boomed out.

Josephus held himself low. "Cannon," replied Josephus, pulling the strap of his shield tighter.

Am'yaviasal gazed off in the direction of the explosions.

"It must be Penellina," Farald said. He was on his knees, shuffling up the line from his position in the back.

Despite his efforts, he was far too loud to be effectively sneaking around in the forest. The other elves that travelled with them scowled at each squeak and clank as he moved to the front. Josephus shared in their frustration.

Farald breathed heavily. "Who else would have a cannon around here?"

Josephus smiled. "I knew she'd come back. She wouldn't leave us in the lurch like that."

"You're right," Farald said, smiling back at him. "Probably went to find Thornton all by herself. She's a brave one tha—"

"—what's a cannon?" Am'yaviasal asked with a frown. "Will it hurt the Bael'nindre?"

Farald grimaced.

"Yeeeaaah," Josephus sucked his teeth. "Hard to say. Depends on where she's pointing it..."

Am'yaviasal eyes widened. Bow in hand, he nocked an arrow to the string. "She wouldn't harm them intentionally would she?"

Josephus looked at Farald and raised his eyebrows, indicating the dwarf should respond.

Farald bulged his eyes slightly back at Josephus.

Josephus said nothing.

Farald sighed. "I'll level with you," he said, facing Am'yaviasal. "She's killed your kind before. But she only did so as a last resort."

"In fact, one of those horrible, snarling, demonic beasts was about to kill me," Josephus said. "She killed it instead. She saved me."

"Yes," Farald nodded eagerly, chuckling. "It's not as though she mass-murdered a whole bunch of them or anything." His chuckle trailed off.

Tears welled up in Am'yaviasal's eyes. He let them flow freely as he stared at the ground. Several of the other elves turned their faces away, and wiped their own eyes.

Am'yaviasal took a steadying breath. "It is regre able, but understandable. She faces no ill will from me or my people. But, we have to help her now, before they force her to kill more."

Finally. An opportunity for a simple, heroic gesture. Josephus stood and pointed his sword in the direction the cannon shot had come from. "We have to move," he called out. "Penny is in danger!"

Leaves and branches whipped against his shield as he charged forward. He stepped to the side, then leapt over a log. With a dash he scooted under a low branch. In his peripheral vision, the vague movements of the elves were still with him. From somewhere far behind came the sounds of Farald struggling to keep up.

The trees thinned out, and Josephus slowed. The barbaric elves were running across the path ahead, from left to right. A few looked back as they ran, shoving into each other to get ahead. He closed the distance and raised his sword, ready to strike down the first elf he could reach.

A hand on his arm pulled him sideways. Losing his balance, he stumbled but continued on. Glancing back, the worried face of Am'yaviasal watched him. Josephus slowed once more. He'd never wanted to kill the elves before, when he first met Penny, but he hadn't been given a choice. Had he? Prophecies had to be fulfilled. He was the Chosen One…

Realisation hit him harder than any foe ever had. He'd killed innocents. True innocents. He wasn't the hero of the story. He came to a stop and lowered his sword, watching as the barbaric elves continued to run past, seemingly unaware of his presence.

Farald caught up, huffing deeply. "What'd you stop for?"

"I think I've realised something about myself, Farald."

"What's that?" Farald raised an eyebrow.

"Am I the villain of—"

Another explosion cracked through the trees, splintering branches and sending leaves spiralling through the air. A second explosion, like an echo, sent three of the barbaric elves crashing to the ground. They lay limp, ten feet in front of Josephus.

Am'yaviasal gasped and stepped forward, reaching a

hand out. One of the Bael'nindre tried to raise itself from the ground, but the lower parts of its body had been torn away in bloody shreds. It snapped something incoherent at them.

Penny emerged from the smoking fragments of the trees. She stood with a leg to either side of the elf, and pointed a cannon at its head.

"No wait!" Am'yaviasal yelled. "Please!"

"Huh?" Penny's shocked face swivelled, then lit up in recognition. "Guys! Am I glad to see you." She left the dying elf where it lay and strode over to them. "Josephus, do you remember all those crazy barbarian elves you had to kill to get the Eye?"

Josephus winced and nodded wordlessly. Keeping his face hidden from Am'yaviasal, he tried to silently urge her to be quiet.

Penny screwed her face up in slight annoyance. "What?" she shook her head. "Anyway, they've like, totally infested this forest. They're everywhere."

Another barbarian elf crashed through the trees just behind Penny. She turned without hesitation and blasted it with the cannon. Bits of elf rained down over the shards of tree stumps. Its head thumped against the ground some way off.

"Whoa-ho-ho," Penny said. "This is so cool." She glanced back at Farald and Josephus. "Do you guys want a turn? I lost the other cannon somewhere, but you can use this one. Hey, who's this dickhead?" She gave a sneer of disgust to Am'yaviasal.

Josephus faced the elf with an apologetic smile.

"They..." Am'yaviasal's face turned into a scowl. "They... what have you done?" He touched his fingertips to his face, and stared at the blood of his kind.

203

Farald elbowed Josephus and gestured out into the forest. "Maybe we should...?"

"Right. Yes." Josephus gave Am'yaviasal a curt bow. He then turned to the other elves all standing in silent shock and bowed to them. "Thanks for your help. I'm sure we can find Thornton from here."

Josephus started to walk away briskly. Farald grabbed Penny and dragged her along.

Penny looked first to Farald and then Josephus. "What's going on? You haven't caught up with Thornton yet?"

"No. Actually, I was hoping you might have an idea where he is?" Josephus asked, keeping a hand on her back and urging her onward.

She jumped over a leg. "No, I've not seen him."

"Stop!" Am'yaviasal cried from behind. "You can't do this! You must answer to Cal'vain."

Farald gave Josephus a questioning look.

"Cal'vain is the elven god."

"Let's just get out of here," Penny said. She turned and fired the cannon up into the trees behind them. Boughs and branches fell over each other as they crashed to the ground. "Run!" She sounded far too much like she was having fun.

She took off into the forest.

Josephus and Farald followed.

They ran for twenty minutes, slowed, then stopped. Farald stood with his hands on his knees, panting heavily. Penny breathed heavily too, but she wasn't half-collapsed like Josephus's dwarven companion.

"I don't think they're following us," she said.

Josephus eyed the greenery around them. "They can blend into the trees."

"No," Farald gasped. "They'd have a acked us by now."

204

Josephus smiled at Penny. "I knew you would have a change of heart," he said. His story wasn't finished, but maybe it was no longer his alone. "I'm glad you've come back."

"What?" She smirked. "No. I got lost. These elf guys captured me."

"You haven't come back because it was the right thing to do?"

"No. The right thing to do was to leave."

They all looked at each other in silence.

"Okay," Penny said. "I'm heading west, I'll follow the sun. Last chance to come with."

Josephus and Farald both shook their heads.

"You guys all set for ge   ing through the tomb?" Penny asked.

"Yes, I think so," Josephus said. "I've done it before."

"So all set with lock picks? I've um, totally got some. You know how to pick a lock, right?"

Farald hefted his hammer. "We'll just break it down," he said.

She nodded at her feet. "Yeah, of course. And like no problems disarming traps?"

Josephus rotated his shoulder in remembrance of the trap he sprung when retrieving the Eye.

"Yep!" Farald said, tapping the telescopic pole strapped to the side of his backpack.

"You're not worried about needing to sneak past any dungeon inhabitants?" She asked hopefully.

"Wellll," Josephus said, thinking about what they might come across. If Am'yaviasal was right about the Bael'nindre being drawn to strong magic, then they were no doubt travelling through the forest on the way to Reirak. There was no telling how many of the barbarian elves could be waiting for them. "You do have a knack for dealing with those elves."

"Alright," Penny said, rolling her eyes. "You twisted my arm. I'll come with you."

FARALD STAYED AT THE BACK of the column, behind Penellina, watching the forest with a keen eye. Every rustle of leaves, every drop of a stick, brought him reeling to face a potential oncoming enemy. Each time though, there was no assailant, no charging elf, nothing except the ever present swaying of branches and dancing of foliage.

"I don't like this," Farald said. "If not the demon-elves then surely the regular elves should be a   acking."

"Shhh," Josephus hissed over his shoulder. "Did you see which way it went, Penny?"

"Yeah," she whispered. "That way." She pointed her dagger in a seemingly random direction.

"You sure?," Farald asked. "I didn't see it go that way."

"I'm sure."

Josephus took a breath. "Alright, let's keep following it. If what Am'yaviasal said is true, those things are drawn to artefacts. It'll lead us right to Reirak."

"And then" — Penellina tapped the cannon strapped to the side of her backpack — "kaboom."

Josephus frowned at her. "There's no need for all the killing, Penny." He turned and started off in the direction she'd pointed.

"That's easy for you to say," she quipped. "They didn't try to eat *you*."

Farald shouldered through low branches, not daring to take his hands off the war hammer. Why did these two need to talk so much? A twig snapped somewhere to their left.

"Did you hear that?" he whispered.

"Hear what?" Penny said, too loudly.

"Shh," Josephus scolded them.

Farald kept scanning the trees, from left to right, then behind them. They were there, he was sure of it.

In a distant tree, a figure stood atop a bough, with one hand on the tree's trunk. It was barely visible, a dark green silhoue e over dark green foliage. Farald could just make out the bow sticking out past the elf's shoulder. "They're watching us," he said simply.

Josephus picked up the pace, mu ering about losing the barbarian elf they followed. Farald frowned, it was far too easy to make a mistake or walk into a trap when you were in a rush. But time wasn't on their side.

A familiar feeling welled up inside him, like an old friend grasping his shoulder in greeting. It ran down his arm and nestled in his fingertips. He flexed his grip on the hammer.

"Wait a moment," he said.

Penellina and Josephus paused.

Penellina rolled her eyes.

Josephus looked at Farald and gave him an exasperated look. "What is it now?"

Farald rested the hammer on the ground and gazed down into his hands. This wasn't the magic of Whurgan. This was something else. It felt more chaotic. No, that wasn't the right word. It felt more *instinctual*. He raised his hands over his head as they emi ed a purple light. An energy silently emerged from his hands and radiated out over the three of them, forming a dome that comfortably surrounded them. Its purple light dissipated, leaving no trace of its existence.

"What was that?" Josephus asked him, eyes wide.

"I think it's a protection spell." Farald shook his head, staring at his hands once again. "Like a shield. But I'm not entirely sure."

Penellina picked up a stick and thrust it like a sword, out toward the trees. Where it would have struck the invisible dome, nothing happened. "I think your 'spell' was a dud."

"Come on," Josephus said. "It's this way."

They pushed through the undergrowth for an hour more. The trees became sparser, struggling to hold onto rocks or push through patches of hard clay. Through the thinning canopy overhead the mountains come into view. He groaned at the prospect of more climbing.

With his watchful eyes moving, Farald shifted his hand on the hammer. If the normal elves were going to a   ack, it would be before they lost the advantage of the trees.

"What's he doing?" Penellina asked.

Farald looked past her at one of the demon-elves with its back to them. It stood next to a large outcropping of rock, a rock which reminded Farald very much of the obelisk in the Ganther Plains. Trees stood like sentinels over it, covering the rock with heavy branches weighed by vines. The elf grunted something.

"What's it saying?" he asked.

"I don't know," Josephus sighed. "They don't speak Elvish."

"Get your stinking paws off me, you damn dirty elf!"

Thornton stumbled into view, followed by a demon-elf wielding a club. The demon-elf they had followed turned and hissed at Thornton, then seemed to bark something at his newly arrived peer. They argued, pointing and gesticulating at Thornton, but clearly speaking to each other.

Looking scared and witless, Thornton stepped

backwards, away from his captors. He didn't seem bound or hindered in any way. Thornton scanned his surroundings. His eyes fell upon Farald, Penellina, and Josephus. With his hand up in the air he made to shout something but stopped himself. He pulled his hand back down to his side and watched the two demon-elves.

With the elves off to one side, Farald had an idea. It wasn't the best idea he'd ever had, but they were running out of time. "Let's just rush them now," he said, stepping forward.

"No, no!" Penellina held her arm out, blocking Farald. "Let me." She pulled her pack around to the ground and got her cannon ready.

Josephus mouthed something and averted his eyes.

Penellina stepped forward, pointing out the cannon to Thornton. She held her fist up, and then blossomed her fingers open.

Thornton smiled and nodded eagerly.

She stepped forward, took aim... and then fell backwards as a spark of purple burst to life a few feet in front of her. A shock wave of energy spread across the invisible curved surface of the protective dome. An arrow fell to the forest floor.

Farald snapped his head to the direction of its source, and spied an elf in a tree, moving to a new position. The elf moved faster than his eyes could track. A second burst of purple bloomed behind Penellina. Another arrow fell. Soon flares of purple ignited the air all around them. Josephus, Penellina, and Farald stood in the centre.

Elves — the normal kind, not the demon kind — had them completely surrounded. None of the a ackers made any effort to camouflage themselves now. There weren't this many elves with Am'yaviasal before, he must have signalled for reinforcements.

Thornton kept his head low and rushed to the dome. He winced as an arrow whistled through his hair.

"No!" Farald shouted, holding his palm out. "Stay back! You'll get hit."

Thornton pulled himself up short. As he did, one of the demon-elves grabbed him and threw him to the ground. The other elf dived on top of him and started tearing at his clothes and — oh god — at his face. Thornton screamed as thick trails of blood splashed across the ground.

Josephus was the first to rush forward, lifting his sword and bringing it down atop the first elf. The blade wedged deeply into the elf's shoulder with a crack. Josephus tried to yank it free. A renewed flurry of arrows spo ed purple all around him.

Farald shouldered the second demon-elf, throwing it off of Thornton. His hammer made short work of it.

The arrows stopped.

"Ugh." Thornton coughed.

Farald got down on his knees by the man's side. He rubbed his hands together vigorously, felt the heat in his skin, and placed his palms on Thornton's bloody and torn body. With his eyes closed, Farald mouthed a prayer.

Nothing happened.

He cursed himself for his idiocy and tried again, with more urgency than before, this time with no prayer.

Nothing happened.

Josephus looked up at Farald in shock. "Do something."

"I can't. I don't know. This isn't the same as Whurgan's magic."

Josephus's eyes dropped to Thornton's. He cupped the

man's head in both hands, and gently turned his face to his. "Why did you send Tho to kill me? Why?! I'd have done anything you wanted."

Thornton's eyelids fell back into his head. His pupils dilated. His rapid breathing stopped, a ra   le of air bubbled through the blood in his mouth. The body remained still.

Josephus looked up at Farald. "Who's the Chosen One now?"

CHAPTER SIXTEEN

Reirak

PENELLINA KICKED JOSEPHUS AND SHOOK Farald. "Come on! Come on! We have to go. The magic shield thing is wearing out."

An arrow struck the ground nearby, well within where the dome previously reached. Farald looked at the arrow in shock, rising to his feet. Josephus stood and intercepted an arrow with his shield.

Penellina darted forward, ducking as close to Josephus as she could. An arrow grazed her arm, she cried out. Farald appeared beside her, half turning his torso to shield her. A line of blood rose along her upper arm.

She shoved at Josephus. "Run! Run!"

They rushed forward in an awkward phalanx. Whichever arrows penetrated the magic shield pinged off Farald's chest plate or Josephus's shield. Penellina looked down at her own lightweight leather armour, and tucked herself in between them.

At the edges of her vision, she caught glimpses of elves dashing between the trees, loosing arrows. One of them swung in on a rope, slashing a thin sword in the air. The dome didn't impede it. Josephus blocked the blade with his own, flinging the elf aside. They didn't stop running. More and more elves filled the space in the forest.

Peeking out from under the bouncing shield, she spied a smudge of darkness in the trees ahead. It was more than just a well-shaded spot or a particularly dense patch. At least, she hoped it was.

"That way!" She leaned into Josephus and pulled Farald in by his belt.

They careened through scrubs and saplings, snapping branches and stems. An arrow flew past Penellina's face, having found a gap in the armour surrounding her. Penellina urged them on faster, half pushing, half being pulled along. She held on for dear life.

The undergrowth was suddenly gone, and blackness swallowed them. Josephus stumbled forward, dragging Penellina down with him. She landed on his back and rolled beyond him. Farald cla ered to a stop nearby. She lifted herself off the floor and felt it spring beneath her. Her hands felt wooden boards.

She stood in a half crouch, unseen arrows ricocheting off the stone while her eyes adjusted to the darkness. From the mouth of the cave, angry silhoue es rushed in, arrows preceding them. One of the elves took aim at Penellina and fired. Her mind froze as the arrow flew toward her. Her limbs felt sluggish.

The boards gave way, dropping her at the moment the arrow was to strike her face. Penellina's side struck dirt at an angle. She barrelled along, end over end, out of control. From above came the clanging of Farald and Josephus falling with her. Her eyes caught dim glimpses of rock, dirt, and then nothing except darkness. As the tumbling slowed, she realised they had fallen through a shaft, and now rolled along a steep ramp, taking them to some lower level.

She came to a rest and groaned, pushing herself to her feet. The darkness had abated. Before she had fully risen, a hand pulled her up and dropped her onto her feet.

"We've got to move," Josephus said, staring past her anxiously. "What are you—?"

—With a crack, Farald's hammer split a wooden beam on the side of the tunnel. Ahead of him the dirt sloped upward to the level above. The roof caved in after the second strike, drowning them in a cloying cloud of dirt and dust. Penellina was dragged along again. Her feet found the floor and pumped furiously to keep pace.

When they reached the edge of the cloud, Josephus slowed and let her go. Farald emerged a moment later, coughing and spi ing. All three of them were covered in dirt. Penellina took a moment to survey their surroundings. They were in a cave, though it was devoid of the usual stalagmites and stalactites she expected. A few support beams, like the one Farald knocked down, were spread out unevenly along the tunnel. With surprise, she realised she could see, though none of them held any light sources. She peered into the darkness at both ends of the tunnel, but there was no obvious source of the diffuse light.

"Where's that light coming from?" she asked.

Farald's mouth hung open. "I—I think it's me," he said.

"Another spell?" Josephus asked. "I'm glad, we're going to need a few more."

"Why did you smash in the cave?" Penellina asked Farald.

"They were right behind us. Seemed like the most

sensible thing to do."

Josephus checked his sword and shield for damage. "Yeah, but those barbarian elves have been a   racted to here. There's no telling how many are already down here."

A scuffling sound came from down the tunnel. Penellina watched the distant darkness, waiting for a wall of barbarian elves to charge them. "What do we do now?"

"Have hope," Josephus said, flourishing his sword. "We're in the Dark Night of The Soul now. All we need to do is persevere, and finish things."

His stupidity pulled her away from her fearful thoughts. "What are you talking about? Dark Souls?"

He shook his head with a rueful smile. "It's the lowest point in the story. Where the hero... *heroes* fear that all hope is lost. But they rally together and achieve their goal."

"I don't feel hopeless," Farald said. "I feel fine. Let's just keep moving."

Farald pulled the telescopic pole from his backpack and walked forward. He tapped the ground in front of them with each step. Only after he struck every suspicious lump of stone or patch of shadow, did he take another step.

They proceeded this way for ten feet before Penellina lost her patience. "Are you fucking kidding me?" she asked. "Whurgan'll take over everything before we get anywhere near Reirak."

"She's got a point," Josephus said. "Maybe we could just sort of... wave it in front of us. I'm the moron in the forest, I am the Chosen One again. The prophecy protects me."

"It doesn't protect me," Farald declared. "Besides, Thornton died. Whose to say you can't die?"

"I think it's a good idea," Penellina said. "It will clear spider webs and stuff."

"Spiders?" Farald studied their faces, his eyes wide. "Subterranean spiders? Do you think there are any down here?"

"There's no telling," Josephus said, looking to Penellina.

Penellina cupped her chin on her thumb and index finger. "Definitely a concern."

Farald nodded and continued forward at a brisker pace. He waved the pole in front of them, being sure to strike both walls, ceiling, and floor. Every clump of freed dirt caused him to jump back in fear and jab the pole at it.

Penellina followed along behind. Josephus bumped Farald a few times to keep him moving.

After fifteen minutes, a corner appeared in the tunnel ahead. A golden glow emanated from beyond it, causing the rocks to glisten and sparkle nearby. It reminded Penellina of the blinding light that came with Whurgan's arrival.

The rock of the wall next to her gli ered. She stepped closer and peered at the rock, running her hand along it. It was previously impossible to tell in the diffuse light of Farald's spell, but now with this additional light, the veins of gold were visible. They curved through the rock in thin, fractal pa erns, occasionally joining together to form a thicker strand. It was everywhere.

"It's a lode," Farald declared, watching Penellina.

Excitement bubbled up from deep within her. She pulled out her dagger and dug at a particularly sparkly, particularly chunky streak of gold. With all her strength she pulled down on the blade, hoping to pry free some form of payment for all the shit she'd been through the last few days.

The knife gave way, sending her sprawling to the floor. She held the hilt of the dagger up to her face. The broken blade sat at the bo om of the wall. The gold appeared untouched.

"Shitsticks," she said. She glanced at Josephus, then back to the wall. "Lemme borrow your sword," she said with her hand held out.

"There's no time, Penny," Josephus replied. "We can come back later. *After* we're done with Whurgan."

Penellina held the cannon up to her shoulder and peered along it at the gold. She flicked the switch, making it click into readiness.

"NO!" Farald yelled. He grabbed the pipe and forced it down. "Don't be daft. You'll bring the whole thing down on top of us."

Josephus gave her a disapproving look and shook his head. He proceeded toward the glow and went around the corner. Farald followed. Penellina gazed at the wall longingly, dusted herself off, and went with them, holding the cannon tightly.

JOSEPHUS STAYED LOW AS HE rounded the corner and entered the hall, unwi ingly making himself as small as the cavern made him feel. The bloom of yellow light illuminated the surrounding walls, revealing thick seams of gold, reminiscent of lightning, streaking and spli ing as they lay across the surfaces. Above him, the ceiling was shrouded in darkness, the glow not strong enough to reach so high.

A hundred feet away, at the other end of the hall, three steps led up a dais, upon which stood a pedestal. Whatever was atop the pedestal was glowing, so vibrantly it hurt to look at directly. Josephus held his shield up to protect his eyes, and stepped forward.

"Guys, I think I know where Reirak is," Penny said. She crept alongside Josephus, staying close to his shield. Her cannon sat tucked in under her arm, her eyes flicked from one direction to the next.

As they continued, Josephus's foot scraped against the rough stone underfoot. Despite the work put into the stairs and the dais, the rest of the cavern appeared untouched by masons. Even the dais itself appeared half finished, with only portions of the edges carved to smoothness and bevelled.

"Remember, it's a trap," Farald said. He collapsed his pole and brought his hammer to the ready. "Whurgan is waiting for something. He's here. I know it." He kept his head on a swivel, surveying the hall.

"Fuckin' show yourself, you ugly beardless dickhead!" Penny cried out.

Josephus stopped and stared as her voice echoed around them. She shrugged. He looked at Farald, but the dwarf had his back to them, holding his hammer, ready for any assault.

Her voice echoed several more times before fading away. Josephus was thankful there was no reply.

"That's what I thought!" she taunted again. "Too busy playing with yourself to do anything about us taking Reirak."

"Penny," Josephus hissed. "I think that's enough antagonising a god. Don't you agree?"

"He's not even here," she said, pushing past and walking forward with her chin up. She raised her arm to shield herself from the light.

Josephus and Farald hurried after her. When she reached the bo om step to the platform, she lifted her foot to it and held it there. She pulled it back again.

"So... Farald?" she asked.

"Yes?"

"Thornton was the Chosen One, but he's dead. And now

Josephus is the Chosen One... again?"

Josephus smiled and stepped forward. *He* was the moron in the forest, definitely. "That's right," he declared. "When Thornton died, the Chosen One status reverted to me."

Farald raised an eyebrow. "'Reverted'?"

"Hear me out," Josephus said. "The prophecies *have* to come true, right? Well, who most meets the criteria for the Chosen One of Azair Soloth, now that Thornton is dead? Me!" He smiled more and held his arms out. It felt good to be the Chosen One again. And it made so much sense: the Dark Night of The Soul was when he *wasn't* the Chosen One, but now he had come to realise he was still an important hero, even without prophecy, and so he had now been rewarded with what he most wanted. The stories all followed the same plot structure.

Farald's mouth opened, and he gazed at the pedestal, then back to Josephus. "You must be right. I can't think of any other way any of this makes sense."

Josephus sheathed his sword, wet his fingers and smoothed his hair. He pulled his armour into position and dusted off his shoulders. Penny gazed up at him. He thought he detected a hint of admiration in her eyes.

"What are you doing?" she asked.

"How do I look?" Josephus asked back.

She rolled her eyes. "Fine."

Josephus turned to Farald and gave him a questioning look.

"You look... fine," Farald said.

With his heart beating and adrenaline pumping, Josephus took to the stairs. This was it. This was the moment his entire life had been building up to. Through the betrayals, the loss of friends, the death of his mentor, he had remained the hero. His steadfastness and courage in the face of insurmountable odds had made him the epitome of heroism, a beacon that shined out from the depths of despair, granting hope to the desperate and downtrodden. Tales would be told of this moment for generations to com—"

"—what are you just standing there for? Hurry up," Penny whined. "It's cold in here and weird. The sooner you take it, the sooner we can go."

He bounded up the stairs. Without breaking his stride, he approached the pedestal, holding his arm across his eyes. The searing light diminished the closer he got. Finally, with his legs by the plinth, he lowered his arm and gazed upon Reirak.

It was small, and thin. No longer than six inches. A jeweller's tool. He'd seen this before, in the void beneath the obelisk of the Ganther Plains. But there was no sculpted hand here, and no Eye.

Josephus took a deep breath to steady his trembling hand. He reached down and touched the hammer. He took it in his fingers and removed it from the pillar.

The light went out, plunging Josephus and the cavern into u er darkness. He turned and peered the way he had come but couldn't make out any details.

"Guys?" he called out. "Are you still there?"

"Hold on a minute," Farald said.

The same odd light that seemed to come from nowhere and everywhere returned. At first it revealed Farald, before spreading out from him, like an expanding sphere, to encompass Penny, the steps, and then finally, Josephus.

Farald gazed in wonder at the surrounding light, shaking his head. His eyes came to a rest on the hammer, delicately held in Josephus's fingertips.

"*That's* Reirak?" he guffawed. "How the hell are we supposed to hit Whurgan with that?"

A deep, commanding voice reverberated in the cavern. "You're not supposed to."

Josephus held his shield at the ready, and Reirak in his fist. The head of the hammer didn't pass his knuckles. Even though it was a deceptively weak weapon, the stories often told of great power seeming weak and small. Just look at Grilk. Josephus frowned.

An orb of white appeared in the darkness of the ceiling, above the centre of the hall. It plummeted, faster than gravity alone would allow for. When it hit the ground it vanished, leaving in its place Whurgan and Mori.

The god stood with his same gorgeous armour, the Eye of Aera si ing prominently in the centre of the breastplate. In his hands, he held the great tower shield and his axe, even more glorious than Josephus remembered.

Mori was similarly adorned in splendid armour. She held a morningstar across both hands, its thick spikes glinting in the light. Her face was set in stone, ready for a fight.

The final ba le!

Josephus wasted no time. He launched himself off the platform and charged the god.

Without thinking, he weaved randomly as he crossed the vast distance. Mori held her hand up, as though she was pointing above Josephus, and then threw it down. A lightning bolt struck the ground just behind him. Again and again lightning struck. The echo of thunder became dense and deafening. He felt the electricity in the air.

He lunged at Mori, then, in the final instant, twisted and threw himself at the god. Whurgan's hammer breezed through the edges of Josephus's hair. He smiled, breathless, as the god overextended himself, moving the shield just as Josephus reached it. Time seemed to stand still as Josephus thrust his hand out, preparing to tap the Eye with Reirak. Just one li le tap and the world would be saved. Just one li le tap and he would be immortalised as a hero.

With the tinniest of sounds, the hammer struck the jewel at the centre of the Eye.

Josephus crashed into the god and fell to the ground. The shield strapped to his arm taking the brunt of the impact. His head whipped up as Whurgan reeled backwards, yelling incoherently, and flailed his axe and shield. Mori's mouth hung open in horror as she reached out to her god.

"HAHAHAHAH!" Whurgan roared. "Oh my *god*! HAHAHA! You actually thought that a li le hammer like that was going to do anything to me?!"

The mirth in the god's face was quickly replaced by anger as he took two strides forward. Josephus felt the impact from the backhand snap his head to the side, but it was nothing compared to the sting of knowing with certainty that he wasn't the Chosen One.

The hammer left his hand and tinked to the stone floor. He sailed through the air and winced as the ground rushed up to meet him.

As Whurgan struck Josephus, Farald reached a hand out, creating a cushion of air that eased the man's descent to the ground. But a grunt escaped Josephus as he hit the stone floor. Something cracked as he rolled along. Farald's fingers still tingled with the magic, even as he tightened his grip on the war hammer.

Before Josephus stopped tumbling, Farald was already

running, head down, glowering at the god. As he reached Whurgan, a voice — no, a thought — told him to change direction. He ignored it, and pressed onward, just as Mori thrashed her hand through the air.

The bolt of lightning struck his shoulder, sending a flash of searing pain through his arm. His fingers convulsed reflexively, and he dropped the hammer. He fell with it, landing on a knee, gripping his now limp arm. Not once did he remove his eyes from the god.

"I will give you one final chance, Farald. Join me. Become my cleric once again, and I will restore you to your proper station. We will bring heaven to earth."

Mori's eyes snapped to Whurgan. She instantly averted her gaze and sneered at Farald.

"No." Farald pointed his finger at the god, and rose to his feet. He ignored the pain flowing through his arm. At least he could feel it again, though it was still useless. "Yours is a broken heaven. A shallow thing, full of indifference for those who suffer, cruelty to those who stumble. I won't be a part of it. I won't be a part of it ever again."

"Fool!" Mori threw both hands down.

Farald jerked his head back as two bolts of lightning came down from an indeterminate point above. They intermingled, twisting around each other like vines, and struck him in the chest. Every nerve in his body screamed in pain, but he gri ed his teeth against it, unwilling to give her the satisfaction.

Once the energy had passed through every part of his body, it accumulated within him. Whatever new magical ability he had now harnessed the lightning, drew strength from it, and then unleashed it.

A white-hot flame burst around Mori. At first she didn't

react, too busy preparing her next a   ack. But the flames licked at her boots, at her chainmail shirt, at the armour encasing her. She screamed in agony, turned to her god, and collapsed to her knees. Her hands reached up.

Whurgan looked down on her in disgust as she pleaded up at him to save her. He made no movements, save to push her away with his boot when she collapsed to her hands. She rolled a short distance, and was still. The white flames died down. Her body looked completely untouched by the fire, but her unblinking eyes stared at the dark above, her chest didn't move.

As Whurgan regarded her remains with his mouth twisted in disgust, Farald a   acked. Holding onto the end of his war hammer's shaft, he spun around. The cave blurred as he moved. With the full weight of his body behind the weapon's momentum, he swung it at the god's head.

The impact was deafening, the shock dropped the hammer from his hands. A crack of thunder that threatened to level the entire underground chamber assaulted his ears. He clutched at his head, fearing his skull would split open. As he fell to his side, he glanced up. Reirak was on the ground in front of him. Beyond it, Whurgan staggered, and dropped his axe to the ground.

Not knowing what else to do, Farald pinched Reirak between his finger and thumb, and tossed it. He knew before he'd let go his aim was true. It struck the Eye at the centre of Whurgan's chest, and then fell to the ground.

The god's eyes fixed on Farald.

PENELLINA WATCHED ON IN HORROR as Whurgan picked up the axe and held it over his head. Farald was doing his best to back away, but he wasn't moving fast enough. Josephus groaned a short distance behind Farald and tried to stand, but he collapsed back to the ground.

There was nothing she could do. What could she do?

From the tunnel they'd used to enter the cavern, a chaotic cavalcade of footsteps sounded. A barbarian elf emerged and paused near the threshold. Mu ering and screeching, his head moved in quick jerks, taking in the surrounding hall.

Whurgan paused in his swing and glanced back. He lowered the axe and faced the elf, tilting his head quizzically. Another elf dashed out of the tunnel and paused next to the first. They jostled with each other for position.

Both of them wore much nicer clothes than Penellina had seen barbarian elves wearing before. Vibrant green tunics and brown trousers, not at all torn or decayed. A third appeared, and then a wall of them flowed in, grunting and chortling.

The first elf's eyes fell on Whurgan. He pointed at the god and hissed. In unison, the other elves faced Whurgan, and all together, they ran at him. More and more elves sprinted into the hall, all of them in a fervour, shoving and bumping each other as they reached out to the god.

Whurgan swung his axe in a wide arc, sending several of the elves smashing into others. He slammed his tower shield to the ground, sending a visible shock wave, six elves deep, into the approaching mass. Despite his efforts, he was soon overwhelmed. The elves piled over him, pulling and tossing each other aside.

The pile exploded in a fury of white light, sending elves and body parts spiralling through the air. Penellina clicked her cannon and readied it. An elf broke off the a ack on Whurgan and lashed out at her. She blasted it across the cave. A second and third elf, knocked toward her by

Whurgan, turned and ran at Penellina. She shot them into pieces.

Whurgan ba led on, beset on all sides by vicious elves. Farald backhanded an elf as he struggled to his feet. His frantic eyes caught Penellina.

"Penellina! Help!" he grunted. An elf knocked him sideways. Another pounced on him.

She rushed forward, clicking the cannon over and over again. Where it was pointed didn't ma er now, only that it wasn't pointed at her friends. They were surrounded by elves. Hundreds of them, all baying for blood.

Josephus appeared by her side and whirled so the backs of his legs were against her. His sword thwacked into elves behind her. They broke against his shield. She continued on, tucking the cannon under her arm as she reached down to Farald. His hand gripped hers and she pulled, arching backwards to get him to his feet.

Farald hefted his war hammer and stepped away from her, swinging it in wide arcs, clearing a path for them to get closer to Whurgan. Every fibre of her being told her to move away, but Josephus at her back, and the relentless elves to her sides, forced her onward. She gri ed her teeth.

One of Farald's mighty swings left a trail of red flame in its arc. The hammer ignited. Red fire reflected in the eyes of the elves as it cracked into them. Penellina kept the cannon blasting away.

Then they were there, standing behind Whurgan as he ba led the elves. He had grown in size, now twice as large as he was before.

Josephus stepped to her side, Farald fell into her other. Her two friends a acked Whurgan in unison, bellowing incoherently. Just as their weapons fell, Penellina activated the cannon.

Whurgan whirled and slammed his shield down. The impact slapped Josephus and Farald aside. It threw Penellina to the ground, causing her to lose her grip on the cannon. It ski ered away, under the feet of the newly encroaching elves.

The god loomed over them.

Reirak rested on the ground by Penellina's face. She gripped it in her small hands and stood. Whurgan's gaze fell upon her and he laughed. He grabbed her by the hair and pulled her off the ground, so her face was level with his.

The god smirked. "You are nothing. You are weak. You are—"

—Penellina tapped the Eye with Reirak.

The gem cracked. Whurgan looked down at his chest. The crack splintered across the gem. A piece fell out. Then it crumbled.

Whurgan's grip faltered, and Penellina landed on her feet, quickly backing away. The god grasped desperately at the pieces of the Eye falling from his chest, then flailed at the world around him. A ray of blinding white light broke through the ceiling, sending boulders of rock crashing down into the elves.

The light fell on Whurgan and engulfed him. His cries of pain and outrage were drowned out by a high pitched whine. Then the light and the noise were gone, taking the god with them. The elves that had surrounded them lay dead, hundreds of them arrayed in piles.

Penellina turned. Josephus and Farald stared at her, their mouths hung open. Farald glanced down at her hand. She looked at Reirak.

"Holy shit," she yelled. "*I'm* the Chosen One!"

CHAPTER SEVENTEEN

The Really Real Chosen One

JOSEPHUS IGNORED HIS BLOND HAIR blowing across his face and smiled at his friends' arrival. The carriage rounded the corner and emerged from the dappled shadows over the driveway, its metallic trims glinting in the midday sun. An elf sat upright, high on the driver's seat, and pulled the horses to a stop in front of the tower.

From the back of the carriage, three well-armed humans hopped down and quickly surveyed the surroundings. Josephus looked on in anticipation. At a nod from one of them, the elf driver climbed down, opened the door to the carriage, and stood to the side.

Farald emerged first. He wore the same armour provided by the Thieves' Guild, but several decorative modifications had been made. Colourful feathers burst from the joint at the shoulder, red and white paint lined the breast-plate. An animal skin hung on his side. He retrieved his war hammer from the back of the carriage.

The elf blew on a short trumpet, providing a sharp

fanfare for the emergence of Penny. She held her chin up, managing to look down her nose at the much taller servants around her. Josephus felt compelled to step back as the bodyguards moved forward.

"Enough!" she declared. "Stand… over there." She pointed toward the road, the guards and driver walked briskly to their assigned position.

Josephus renewed his smile. "Welcome, Farald. Welcome, Penny. Lunch is wait—"

"—*Queen* Penellina to you." Penny held a finger up.

"Knock it off," Farald said. "You're not royalty."

"Doesn't ma er," Penny said. "I'm as rich as royalty."

They climbed the steps and entered the tower.

At first, Josephus assumed there would be some trouble in securing Master Thornton's previous residence for himself, but after clearing out what was valuable, his former master's real children had no wish to live in the building. 'Too inconvenient' they had said, preferring their more illustrious abodes in Orthendine. Josephus got it for a good price.

As they ascended the stairs to the upper level, he took them in. Farald stepped lighter and seemed more energetic. Purpose had rekindled the fire and passion in the old cleric. Penny stepped as though she belonged in these wealthy surroundings, stepped as though the tower's lordly position in the centre of Threerun was too low for her.

They sat on a balcony on the upper level, overlooking the river, boats, and sailors going about their days. Men called to each other as they directed the unloading of a ship.

"Well friends," Josephus said. He paused, watching them, then turned back to the water. What more was there to say? "I can't believe you were the Chosen One all along, Penny."

He shook his head wryly.

"From what I've been told, she wasn't *always* the Chosen One," Farald said. "Just so happened that she was the moron in the forest."

Penny held a finger up. "I think," she declared. "That I *was* the Chosen One from the *beginning*, and I was *always* the Chosen One. I just didn't know it."

"You could have been," Farald chuckled. "Who really knows?"

"Well," she said. "Like *you* told us, the gods have a funny way about them. A priest, a thief, a warrior... a wizard." She looked down at her hands.

Josephus smiled and turned to Farald. "How is Grilk by the way? Is he enjoying being a deity?"

"Doing well considering how new it all is," Farald nodded. "He's ge ing a handle on his new responsibilities."

Penny put her feet up on the railing. "What's it like up there?" She gazed up at the sky.

Farald tilted his head side to side. "He hasn't quite figured everything out. But he said he'd come say hello when he's worked out how to appear in visions."

"Does he get, like, training?" Penny asked. "I found there's a lot of rules for being royalty. Hard to keep track."

Farald frowned a li le. "Well, some of the other gods are helpful. Some less so."

"I imagine Whurgan is causing him some trouble?" Josephus mused.

"Well, that one's in a bit of hot water from what Grilk tells me. 'Meddled' too much, broke the rules."

It was good Grilk was doing well. It went a long way to smooth over the sharp pangs of guilt Josephus still felt when thinking about how he treated his friend. "What are you going to do, Queen Penny? Does the royal life not suit you?"

She cocked an eyebrow at him and made a dagger appear in her hand. "I've got a bit more to learn from Galan and Grog. But they say I've got the knack of things. They've never been asked to train a queen before. I bought Reirak back from them."

"Thank you," Farald said. "The Vuhsi and I will keep it safe."

Her gaze fell to the ground. "But you know... I don't much like being a queen. It's hard work. I think I'm going to go soon, buy a ship and a crew, go see Palaencia." She smiled to herself. "I'll leave a steward in charge."

Josephus looked over Penny's head to Farald. "And what of you, High Priest? Where are you ordered to next?"

"My... flock is waiting for me, out on the plains," he replied. "Muchok has gathered all of the Vuhsi. They are eager to meet me and show me our home." His eyes gazed into the sky. "I've found my clan."

Josephus nodded. "And the rumours of war?"

Farald sighed. "They're true. The elves are all riled up. They believe Whurgan to be responsible for all the elven deaths in the Direwood. Having the dwarven armies ready for a war hasn't helped. Some diplomats are running about, trying to ease tensions, but Dwon and Norim have somehow secured themselves positions of influence. War is coming to the mountain homes."

They sat in silence as a ship sailed under the bridge below them. A group of children ran alongside the riverbank, jumping and waving at the sailors.

"And you?" Farald asked.

"I... I don't know. Not being the Chosen One gives me a certain amount of freedom."

"So does all that fucking gold from the cavern," Penny pointed out.

Josephus sighed. "Yes. I guess my story isn't finished. But I think it might be a li le dull from now on. I'm going to build an orphanage, and rebuild the Black Dog. And if I never see another prophecy again, I'll die happy."

Penellina snorted. "You never know. You can't prevent prophecy."

Thank you for reading You Can't Prevent Prophecy!

I am planning on additional stories in the same style and in the same world. If you'd like to know more, you can sign up to my mailing list at https://dgredd.net and I'll send you an email when they are published, or when any other works by me are released.

If you enjoyed this story, I would really appreciate it if you could leave an honest review on Amazon. It helps to increase visibility so that other people can enjoy my stories. If reviews aren't your thing, I'd love to hear what you think at info@dgredd.net.

Once again, thanks for reading. I hope that you enjoyed my story.

With thanks,
D.G. Redd